Everstille's Librarian

A Novel

Susan M. Szurek

Book Two: A story from the town of Everstille

Chapbook Press

Schuler Books
2660 28th Street SE
Grand Rapids, MI 49512
(616) 942-7330
www.schulerbooks.com

Everstille's Librarian, A Novel

ISBN 13: 9781948237673

eBook ISBN: 9781948237697

Library of Congress Control Number: 2020924387 (Paperback edition)

Printed in the United States by Chapbook Press.

For Connie Jo...

always understanding and accepting

Also by Susan M Szurek:

Everstille: A Novel

There is no greater agony than bearing an untold story inside you.

Maya Angelou

Names

Names are strange things. Some names are obvious and understandable. For example, *Jensen's Hardware and Agricultural Needs* is owned and run by the Jensen family. *Jamison's Livery Stable and Funeral Services* is handled by Mr. Jamison and his sons and has been forever. Likewise, *Clampet's Groceries* and *Peterson's Bakery* are managed by those families. Even *Mitchell's Emporium and Dry Goods* has the family name in its elegant title. And all those establishments are on or near *Main Street*, which is the main street in the town. Easy.

Other names are not so clearly logical. The town's name, *Everstille* was either named by one of the founding families who came from some place in France (or maybe Germany, depending upon who is telling the story) called the same, or it was a nod to the moonshiners whose stills could be easily found if you knew exactly where to look. Some think that somehow the final *e* of the name lends credence to the founding family from France (or Germany) story. But Sheriff Samms, who knows where most of the stills were and are, just nods his head and allows others to continue the discussion, which, on a warm, late summer day drinking lemonade at Mazie's, is as good a discussion as any. By the way, *Mazie's* is dubbed that after the owner, Mazie.

And then there are those places which have names with no easy explanation, like *North Cemetery* which is a couple miles down the west road out of town. Of course, it is on the north side of the road which may account for the name. There was some talk for a while, of renaming it *Jamison Cemetery* after the man whose family owns the gloomy business and administers the sad activities there, but even Mr. Jamison did not want it named after his family. It remains North Cemetery, and most of Everstille's departed citizens have found an eternal home in its expanding boundaries. The Jamison family does have the monopoly on the burial business.

The road west of town was renamed when the Indiana County Board decided to make the country roads easy and logical to locate. The road is officially called *County Road 8.* But many Everstille citizens, especially those who have lived in the area most of their lives, still call it by its original appellation: *Smokehouse Road.* The reason for the original name is undetermined and is no more apparent than the reason for the town's name. It had been suggested that there was a smokehouse somewhere in the area where meat from various animals, both wild and domestic, were smoked. This sounds rational, but no one knows for sure.

Smokehouse Road (or County Road 8) runs east and west, and the eastward path swerves off to several smaller lanes while the main road continues into Everstille where it becomes *Main Street* and runs through the town. If you start at the far end of North Cemetery and work eastward toward the town's Main Street, down County Road 8 (or Smokehouse Road), you will pass quite a few wooded areas and farmlands and paths. One path travels through a copse and ends up in a clearing where a cabin stands. For years the cabin was inhabited by a Mr. Harvey, who under strange circumstances, abandoned the property. His cabin was eventually bought by a man named George Winter, and then the Wells family, who were in some way related to George, moved there. Farther eastward was a small house with a shed and out-building which was the home of Ethel and Samuel Pinkerton and their children: Ernestine, Gladys, and Tobias. Eventually that house was sold to the Jaspers. East of the cemetery and set back from the main road was the Martin farm, and next to it, the Rivens farm. East of the Rivens farm, down an oak-lined path and into the woods just outside the main town was a shack. Shack is the term for it, although it was still habitable and two older brothers, fraternal twins lived there. Nowhere is there any evidence of a smokehouse.

My own name, Anne Olivia Rivens, has a story. Both my great-grandmothers were named Anne, or at least a form of the name. One was *Anna* and the other was *Annette*, so I guess my parents thought that Anne with an *e* was a good compromise. I know the history of Everstille because I grew up there. My parents are Jena and David Rivens, and I grew up with my siblings: David Jr., Raymond, Elizabeth, and Joshua. The older fraternal twins who lived in that shack were my great-uncles, Jake and Lem, and I knew most of the families: the Wells, the Jaspers, the Pinkertons, who lived in the area. I am the youngest child in the Rivens family; Everstille is my hometown; Smokehouse Road is where I spent my youth; and the first part of this story is mine.

Anne Rivens

Harrison Greenwood Memorial Library

Everstille's public library is officially named the *Harrison Greenwood Memorial Library*, and those letters are carved in the stone facade above the wide double door. Obviously, it was named after Harrison Greenwood who has been dead for years. Since 1890, in fact. The library itself is currently found in a newly renovated building. Originally, the library began as a Reading Room housed in the large meeting room at the back of the first floor of the Everstille Methodist Episcopal Church.

Harrison Greenwood died of a massive heart attack brought on, so some claim, by a series of arguments with Mrs. Greenwood. A lovely funeral service at the church was followed by a catered luncheon at the Greenwood home. To further honor him, the wealthy Greenwood family supplied the books for the Reading Room from Harrison's personal library, and the sizeable sum of $750 which furnished the Reading Room with necessary chairs, tables, lamps, and bookcases. It was rumored that Mrs. Greenwood despised their home library because Mr. Greenwood spent most of his days there sipping his imported brandy and eluding her. After his death, after she bequeathed his books to the church, after she endowed the reading room, she turned his expansive library space into the indoor greenhouse she originally wanted. Theirs was a marriage of *inconvenience*.

The Greenwood Reading Room grew in content but not in size. It became the fashion to donate books to the room to honor various deaths, births, marriages, some confirmations, and the occasional birthday. Soon the books were piled on the tables, the shelves, and the chairs of the room, and there was no discernible order to them. In 1905, it was decided to move the library from what had become a crowded, rarely used room to a small, empty house, owned by the Greenwood family, and close to the Everstille Public School at the west end of Main Street. The townspeople were pleased when it officially opened as an actual library. All were convinced that it would improve the minds of Everstille's school children who may have wanted to read ancient histories, religious tracts and texts, and the four volumes of St. Thomas Aquinas' *Summa Theologica*, although no one was sure how that set got into the personal library of a Methodist.

A group of civic-minded women from the Methodist Episcopal Church formed a club, calling themselves the *Rachel Circle*, and made their first duty the organization of the Greenwood Library according to the newly developed and highly respected Dewey Decimal System. They visited the cities of Elkhart and South Bend, wandering around, viewing the stacks in the public libraries there, and discussing with the librarians how to interpret the Dewey System for their own small library. Afterwards, a fashionable lunch was *de rigueur*. Once the empty building was renovated and modified, and the books moved and shelved, the Rachel Circle volunteered, on a rotating basis, to be librarians and keep the library open to the public on Monday, Wednesday, and Friday from 10:00 A.M. until 2:00 P.M. This was not particularly helpful in the education or the elucidation of either the schoolchildren or the general populace of Everstille. And the donation of books continued.

The year 1915 saw some important changes to Everstille's public library system. The Rachel Circle had done their duty in manning the place and went *en masse* to the Everstille City Council meeting not once, but three times, to ask, no, to demand that their hard work not go to waste just because they had voted and decided to end their conservatorship. It was time for the city of Everstille to take ownership and hire a librarian to work there. A connection was created with students at various local colleges and universities, and a series of men (and even a few women) were hired to work at the library. The City Council even found some funds to help expand the small building, and two meeting rooms were constructed. Eventually, the City Council and other civic groups would hold their meetings there.

The advent of the semi-professional librarians allowed the library to open five days and some evenings. It was closed on Mondays, but Saturdays from 9:00 A.M. until noon were particularly busy. That was when many of the farmers and their families came into town to do their weekly shopping. The library books were free to borrow, and *free* was always appreciated. Books continued to be donated and purchased, and the substantial children's section was growing in popularity. The series of Andrew Lang fairy books proved to be so popular that a second and then a third set needed purchasing. Part of the reason was that the books sometimes were not returned, but were kept, cherished, under small pillows. Frank Baum's novels, and Howard Pyle's tales of the Arthurian Knights circulated, and Rudyard Kipling's *Just So Stories* also required multiple copies. By the late 1920's, the Greenwood Library was one of the most popular places in Everstille although St. Thomas Aquinas' *Summa Theologica* remained in dusty loneliness, unopened and unborrowed in Dewey's 200's.

When the Depression hit, it was difficult for the semi-professional student-librarians to maintain even a partial presence in the town, so librarian duties were handed back to the Rachel Circle, and the accessible days and times were, once again, limited. Sometime in the late 1930's, Doctor Emmanuel Evans, the town's esteemed physician, came to a City Council meeting with a proposal and possible solution. His oldest brother's oldest daughter, Ruth, was looking for something meaningful to do. While she had attended a local college for two years, the money was not available for her to complete the education, so she was obliged to return home and was unhappily anticipating life as a spinster. She was young, and her sad letters to her favorite uncle broke his heart. He wanted to do something for her. If the Everstille City Council would hire her, at lower wages given that she was not a college graduate and was a woman, she would be delighted to become the librarian, and she could, until something else came along, live with him. And so, Miss Ruth Evans, now twenty-three, moved to Everstille to take the job as town librarian. She remained in that position for many years. Until I took over.

Ruth Evans was what some people called *mousy*. She was tall, and thin, and wore her brownish hair back in a knot, and if she had one beauty about her, it was her eyes. They were as green as deep summer grass, an unusual occurrence in a brunette, so people said. She was graciously tolerant of the townspeople although she did not easily make friends.

The job was a godsend to her, removing her from the dullness and dislike of her family who lived in an even smaller village than Everstille, and saving her from increasingly frequent arguments with her father. She was the oldest of five, all girls except for the one treasured boy, and she had to beg and plead and work for her chance to continue an education after the twelfth year of schooling she was graciously allowed. She applied for and received a partial college scholarship which allowed her a partial college education.

It was not that Ruth was dismissed by her parents, but one less unmarried daughter to worry about eased her father's mind. Without too much apprehension, Ruth moved with her suitcases and bags filled with books into the home of her uncle and was grateful to have her own space, unshared with younger siblings with whom, frankly, she did not get along. Doctor Evans lived in a lovely old Victorian house which contained several bedrooms and a bathroom on each of the two floors. Ruth moved into the largest bedroom on the second floor and became her uncle's occasional hostess and companion.

Miss Evans took charge of the Greenwood Library and organized that space, spending many more hours there than she was paid to do. She experienced joy at having moved away from an annoying family situation and delight at living in the lovely home with her favorite uncle. But the library became her real home. She planned and ordered and structured and arranged it.

Ruth expanded the inadequate fiction section and encouraged the reading of it. Books by authors like Willa Cather, Agatha Christie, Katherine Mansfield, and Pearl S. Buck, found their equal space among those of Zane Grey, Booth Tarkington, Ernest Hemingway, and Theodore Dreiser. Equality, bestowed by a woman librarian without any fuss or controversy. The reading citizens of Everstille were discreetly schooled in restrained feminism with a skill borne from male confrontations. Ruth Evans relished her job.

The library flourished under her watch. She safeguarded the manuscripts, old and new; she organized and ordered reading and research material; she, surreptitiously, through her quiet encouragement and authentic suggestions, taught the schoolchildren to appreciate the written word. She eased into the life of Everstille, and the citizens benefitted from her benign proprietorship of the books and the library. So, her subsequent romance and eventual marriage, when it did happen, was accepted by all, and thought to be her due. Of course, there was much that people suspected and more that they did not know. I knew some of it because I worked with her and learned some of the secrets. I will tell what I know in due time, but first, about me.

About Me

The earliest memories I have are of me sitting on my sister Elizabeth's lap while she read her schoolbooks out loud. Lizzie is nine years older than me, and I must have been three or four, so she would have been in seventh or eighth grade. She would read while moving her finger along the line of print, then stop and point to some of the words.

"What is this word, Anne? Right there. I just read it. It starts with the *L*-sound."

"*Land,*" I would say, and Lizzie would kiss my head and say, "Yep. Now spell it out. Tell me the letters." And I would.

I assume this is how I learned to read. I don't ever remember not knowing how to, and while we did not have many books meant just for children in our house, there were several history books and McGuffey readers which my older siblings had used to become literate. We had two *Bibles* and a large *Webster's Dictionary*. Charles and Mary Lamb's *Tales from Shakespeare,* and some novels were housed in a small bookcase in our parlor; and the books, when not being read, were kept carefully dusted. Every now and then, another book would find its way into the collection my mother called *The Library.*

My father had completed an eighth-grade education, but my mother went through grade ten, and her enduring joy from her schooling was reading. She said the one regret in her life was not being able to earn a high school diploma, and she was determined that all her children would. We did, although she often alleged that the diplomas my two older brothers earned were rightfully hers due to the continual urging and persuading she used on both Davie and Ray to get them to complete their schoolwork and get to classes. Sometimes the nurturing she communicated to them took a physical form. Every Sunday afternoon, Mother had her own private "reading time", and she shooed all of us, and that included my father, out of the parlor so she could spend an hour or so with her books.

So, I was, and am, a reader. Had any money been available, I would have attended college, but that was not possible. As I became older and found my way to the town's library both after school and on Saturdays, I gave myself as much of an education as I could. When I became friends with Miss Ruth Evans, and later, when I began to work at the library, she taught me by guiding my reading and questioning me about the books she encouraged me to read.

We discussed the books from Harrison Greenwood's collection which no one ever borrowed. I read and struggled through Homer, Herodotus, Sophocles, Plato, and Aristotle. Marcus Aurelius' *Meditations* impressed and influenced me, and I still reread his inspiring words and axioms. I found Thomas More and Martin Luther dry and difficult, but the real Shakespeare plays (not just *Julius Caesar* which was required reading in grade eleven) were so much more exciting than the Lamb's book from my mother's collection, that I never again read Charles and Mary's filtered work. Had my mother known what Defoe's *Moll Flanders* and Cleland's *Fanny Hill* taught me, she would have torn the books out of my hands and forbidden me to go anywhere near the library in town. This was the joy and the pleasure I had in reading: I was educated; I explored; I experienced, and without ever journeying farther than Chicago, I consider myself well-traveled. At least in my mind.

But books and reading were not my only enjoyments. I grew up on the farm and loved being outside. I trailed behind my sister and youngest brother, Joshua, while they fed the chickens and cleaned the barn, and they shepherded me in those tasks. My two older brothers, Davie and Ray, helped Dad with the cows and the crops we grew, and when they allowed, I followed them around and did the inconsequential tasks they didn't want to complete: pulling the weeds, raking through the hay, running back and forth to the house to bring them whatever they decided they needed. Of course, once I grew older and realized this was just busy work to keep me occupied and out of their way, I kept to the house and to the tasks given to me by Mother.

Our farm butted up against the Martin's farm. Their land was sizable and wrapped around the back of ours and out to the side where it met the old Smokehouse Road. The Martins had plenty of cattle, and those animals liked to wander to the fence by that road. Down the oak-lined path was the shack where my mother's uncles lived, and they sometimes helped the Martins with their cows because, strangely enough, those animals were attentive to them, and followed them like our dogs followed Dad. Those oak trees had some low branches, and I learned to climb up into them with a book and spend some time doing the two things I enjoyed most.

Because three of my siblings, Davie, Ray, and Lizzie, were so much older, they went on with their lives, and I did not have much to do with them. Davie and Ray married and moved to the farms of their in-laws. Lizzie married a farmer friend of Ray's and moved with him. Eventually Joshua married one of the Wells' girls, Beatrice, and built a house not too far from ours. But for a while, when were we young, Josh, who was only three years older, and I played together. There weren't many girls my age who lived close to us although I would periodically see one of the Wells girls, Hazel or Ester. The Wells family kept to themselves mostly, and while I sometimes was in a class with one or two of them, we were never close.

Consequently, I was a singular child. I read. I ran outside. I climbed trees and sometimes played with Josh. I spent as much time with Mother as she had for me, asking her questions, begging her to teach me to play our old out-of-tune piano, and avoiding the chores she assigned as best I could. But mainly, I was alone. That is not to say that I was lonely. I was not. I am not sure I knew what loneliness was until the death of Ruth Evans. But that part is not yet to be told. And hers was not the first dead body I had seen. The first were the bodies of my great uncles, Jake and Lem, and that happened the summer I was eleven.

The Summer I Was Eleven

My great-grandmother, the one named *Anna*, had five children; the older three were girls, and the youngest were fraternal twin boys. My grandmother was her youngest daughter, and the boys were her twin brothers, Jacob and Lemuel, who were born, as I overheard my mother explaining to Lizzie, as *change-of-life babies*. Grandmother's brothers were born after she turned twenty, was married and had her own family started, and the twins were both a surprise and an embarrassment for the entire family, especially their three older sisters. When my own mother was born, the twins were already twelve and were living at home with recently widowed Great-Grandma Anna. Jake and Lem attended the local schoolhouse, but because they were what was euphemistically called "simple", it was decided that they were better off staying at home and helping their aging mother with the household chores. They had both learned to print their names, do simple arithmetic, read a bit, and that was the extent of the educational proficiency garnered during their six years of formal schooling.

I'm not sure what the real reason was for Jake and Lem living in the shack out on Smokehouse Road after Great-Grandma Anna died. I was told they put up a fuss when Mother and Dad wanted them to stay in our upstairs third floor bedrooms, and that had something to do with their living arrangements. They moved out to the shack east of our house and down the oak-lined path and seemed to be happy there. After every winter, when the snow disappeared, and the sun launched, Dad and my older brothers would go out to the shack and spend time fixing up what the harsh winter had marred. Sometimes shingles blew off the roof, or the front porch needed new planks. Once the entire front door needed to be replaced, and another time the chimney needed patching. Mother always made sure there were some hardy tomato seedlings and a few other vege-tables for Jake and Lem, and they enjoyed the planting and were good at tending their garden.

Mother and Dad would drive out monthly to pick up the uncles and take then into town to get groceries and needed odds and ends, and as I was the youngest, I was included. We visited Mitchell's Emporium for necessary clothing or shoes, if money was available, and I loved go-ing there. The place was a wonder. The enormous glass display of what seemed like a million types of candy as you entered the store fascinated both the uncles and me, and we each left with our own small white bag of treats. The Mitchell family, who owned and operated the store, were kind; they always saved remnants of cloth they could not sell to give to the uncles who were taught by their mother to weave, braid, and knot scraps of material into colorful and practical rag rugs. The completed rugs were offered for sale at the Emporium, and most of the homes in Everstille had a rug or two warming parts of their wooden floors. Every room in our house had one. In this way, the uncles were able to help support themselves. Knowledge of higher math and the literature of the ancients not needed.

Jake and Lem were inseparable. I never saw one without the other, and when they walked together, Jake was in front and Lem would be behind him. Mother said it was because Jake was born about ten minutes before Lem and was the older brother and the leader. She had an explanation for everything. She explained that the reason the Martin cows followed the uncles around like they did was due to the uncle's gentle and placid natures. The cows did not fear them since they were nonthreatening; they trusted them like our dogs trusted Dad. I knew this to be true because I had witnessed it for myself.

One late spring afternoon caught me sitting in the leafy tree leaning against the dependable branches, watching the cows grazing in the fields across the road, and rereading a book of Edgar Allan Poe stories. I glimpsed a movement and saw the uncles begin to walk down the road towards me, but I was hidden high in the tree and kept still. Jake was in front and Lem, as usual, was behind as they moved a few feet past the oak camouflaging me. They crossed to the fence where Martin's cows were munching and stood there quietly until the nearest cow stopped chewing and slowly turned around and ambled over to them. Another cow came to the fence, and then another until they had queued up waiting for Jake and then Lem to place a hand between each cow's eyes and rub. Then the uncles stepped back on the road and resumed their walk. The cows and I watched them travel about fifty feet. They stopped. Jake turned. I had not moved and was concealed, but I could not shake the feeling that he was looking directly at me in the tree. They continued down the road, and I stayed motionless until they disappeared around the turn. Even now, years later, the entire scene retains a dream-like quality.

That summer before I turned twelve is vivid in my memory for three reasons. First, one of the Wells girls, Rebecca, had disappeared and the town and surrounding areas could gossip about little else. There was some talk about one of the many tramps in the area abducting her. I was present, and then chased out of the room, when Sheriff Samms came to speak to my father about it. A rumor was spreading about the uncles knowing something about Rebecca's disappearance, and Sheriff Samms wanted my dad to go with him to the uncles' shack and ask some questions. They went. The speculation about the uncles proved to be just that. However, everyone was upset and looking for any answer.

Mother was distraught at this news and did what most of the other mothers in town did…forbid their children to pursue their usual summer activities. I was made to stay within the boundary of the house and yard and could only go into town or anywhere else if someone accompanied me. And since everyone was busy with work, and chores, and readying for Lizzie's fall wedding, I spent the summer moping. Time passed slowly. There were just a handful of days until the fall school session would begin.

One dull Saturday afternoon, Mother delegated me to take a basketful of canned foods and baked goods to the uncles' shack. Mother cautioned that I should go there directly and return immediately with the empty basket. I picked it up and ran a short way, but the container proved heavier than I thought, and I had to slow to a fast walk. As I set off down the familiar road, everything seemed to take on an unusual gloominess and gruesomeness. The familiar path seemed longer and more serpentine. The once kindly oak trees stretched evil limbs to the cloudy, overcast sky, and I sensed gooseflesh on my arms. Even the herd of placid cows seemed to render foreign meanness, creating strange shivers. My attempt at fast walking was cut short when I stumbled on a rock and fell to my knee scrapping it. With the blood from the cut running down my leg, and the basket getting heavier and more cumbersome by the second, I limped down the winding lane towards the shack.

When I reached the shack, the uncles were not in sight. I called out their names and hearing nothing in reply, I placed the basket on the front porch, pounded on the door with both fists, and yelled again. Maybe it was the talk of the missing girl, or the Edgar Allan Poe stories I had been reading, but I was anxious, and, leaving the basket, charged back down the road towards home and safety. Later, Mother asked if I had returned the basket to the kitchen. I had forgotten about it and told her I had left it on the porch, and she said we would take a ride after Sunday church and pick it up.

Sunday brought additional dreary weather. We went to church and after the service was over, rode in silence to the shack. We rumbled past the oak trees and the cow pasture where no cows could be seen. As we neared the gravel path, we saw the basket by the front door where I left it. Animals had gotten into it, and the jars were overturned and broken, and the baked goods were destroyed. It was obvious that my uncles had not touched it. Dad stopped the car, and we all sat for some seconds staring at the ruins. There was a quiet about the place that was odd, and Dad directed us to stay in the car while he investigated. He walked up the path calling out to my uncles, then knocked on the door and yelled again. When no one answered, we watched as he turned the doorknob, pushed heavily, and went in. It seemed like forever, and just as Mother started to get out of the car, Dad appeared and motioned to her. She hurried to the house telling me to stay put.

I sat in the car for what seemed an eternity but was probably closer to a minute, and then I opened the car door, walked to the shack, and went in. I had never been anywhere in the shack except for the elongated front room, and since my parents weren't there, I assumed they were at the back in the bedroom was which was where I went. I had never seen a dead person before and certainly had never seen two dead people at once. But it was not the sight of my uncles lying on their bed that was so startling. It was not the tableau of Uncle Lem clutching, in a death grip, the shirt of Uncle Jake that held the unbelieving attention of my parents. It was the bedroom itself.

There were cows everywhere. These cows were crudely cut out of remnants of material, and their tails, udders, and ears were apparent. It was the sheer number of them that was spellbinding. There were calico cows in all patterns. There were cows cut from red brocade and orange broadcloth and white muslin. There were beige canvas cows and dark-green burlap cows and baby-bunting cows. And they covered the walls and the doors and the ceiling. A circle of tea-dyed cheesecloth cows danced around the bed, and brown and navy corduroy cows covered the quilt, having been sewn on rudely with large loopy stitches. In one corner, on an old rocker, were stacks of brightly colored cows waiting to be nailed up with the rest of the herd. They would not be joining them now. A pile of colorful scraps was stacked in another corner with scissors on top. This pile would remain forever just material. There would be no transformation.

We stood in a group and watched in fascination for minutes. Finally, my parents noticed me there, and Mother sent me back to the car. In a while, they returned to the car too. Dad drove me home, and then my parents left to take care of my great-uncles.

A few days later there was a quiet ceremony for Uncle Jacob and Uncle Lem at the North Cemetery. Heart issues, explained Mother to those who asked; yes, both of them. I am not sure what happened to their created herd of cattle, but it was never mentioned by my parents.

A couple weeks after the funeral, Dad and my brothers went to their place, removed any useful items, and tore the old shack down. I guess it was not worth saving. Or maybe it was, but the strangeness of it all needed to be gone.

***

The death of the uncles was the second reason I remember that summer. The third happened just after the fall school session started. Before leaving for school that first full day, I told Mother I was going to stop at the Greenwood Library and would be home a little later. I had read and reread all the books at home and was in need of additional material, so I was going to check out the two books per week I was allowed.

When I entered the library, none of the Rachel Circle women who had played librarian were there. Instead there was a woman I had never seen who was busy organizing and stacking books behind the main desk. I had no idea at that time that this tall woman with the medium length mouse-brown hair pulled into a knot at the back of her neck, and startling green eyes would become so important to me. I did not know at that time that years in the future, the next dead body I would be close to would be that of Ruth Evans, the new librarian.

Ruth Evans, the New Librarian

Ruth Evans brought orderliness and methodology to Everstille's Harrison Greenwood Memorial Library. She maintained uniformity and neatness and did so without any of the bellowing and disinterest the patrons of the library had come to expect with the college imitation-librarians or the Rachel Circle women who were performing the job as duty. Now, when asked where a certain book was, or where to find some specific knowledge, Ruth Evans did not just point an indifferent finger and say "Over there", but with a smile and a wave of her hand would take the person directly to the place, and pull out the book, or help find the information. How she so quickly learned where everything was in the expanding library was a wonder. She was proficient and professional and proper without making anyone feel silly or stupid or slug-like. I admired her.

She soon began to recognize me because I spent so many hours in the library, and she nodded her head in greeting when I walked in. While the library regulations limited me to borrowing two books a week, there was no limit on the number of hours I could remain, or the number of books I could read while there. I had my own system. I would return my two books and rapidly decide which new ones I would borrow, and then chose the additional one I would read while in the library. I had a favorite place towards the back of the stacks where I could hide and read the book in peace. It took several visits to complete a book, so I would mark the page with a piece of colored paper I found, and then hide the book. I hid the book for two reasons. For one, I did not want anyone to borrow it until I finished it, and secondly, I was reading books I chose from the *Adult Section*.

I visited the library most weekdays after school. On Saturdays, I would rise early, rush through my chores, and travel the fifteen minutes it took to get to the library from our farm at a loopy run, clutching the books to be returned. The place opened at nine A.M., and by the time I got there, closer to ten A.M., it was crowded with the farm families who traveled into town most weekends. Because the library closed at noon on Saturdays, I had two hours to read in peace. These hours were the highlight of my week.

One Saturday in early fall, I got a late start. Mother had more chores than usual for me because Lizzie was getting married in a month, and the wedding luncheon would be on our farm. I did not get to the library until much later and had only about forty minutes to spend there.

I returned my books, quickly found two which I checked out, and went directly to the spot I had hidden my *Adult Section* book. I took it out, found a place in the crowded room to settle down, and opened to the page I had marked. A note fell out. It said:

> *Anne Rivens,*
> *Please see me when you receive this.*
> *We need to talk.*
> *Ruth Evans, Librarian*

I was horrified. What was I going to do? Would my privileges be suspended? Would I be thrown out of the library? Was there an arrest in my future? I considered sneaking out of the building, but then what? How could I ever return? I could pretend I never saw the note, but what if Miss Evans stopped me and asked? Should I go to her now? I peeked around the corner and saw she was busy with a line of book-borrowers in front of her desk. I looked at the large clock behind the desk and saw that there were only ten minutes left until the library closed. I had not read any of my book. I was too nervous. I placed the marker back in the book and put it into the hiding spot. I picked up the two books I had checked out and waited until the library was almost emptied before I discreetly and inconspicuously walked to the door. It was crowded, and I thought I would just sneak out with the last large group. As I tried to blend in with those who were leaving, I heard my name.

"Hello, Anne Rivens! Come on over here, please. I need to speak with you."

I looked over to where Ruth Evans was standing. She did not look angry, but there was no smile on her face either. I hesitated and considered pushing my way through the crowd and running home, but then, I knew, I could never return. Besides, Miss Evans knew who I was and what I looked like. She had all my personal information on a little card in that small box on the Circulation Desk, and Sheriff Samms knew me and my family. I might as well take my punishment now. I would be sorry to miss my only sister's wedding and hoped she could slip me a piece of the wedding cake behind the prison bars. When my twelfth birthday came in a couple months, I would be wearing those black and white striped prison outfits I noted in one of the movies Josh and I had seen at the Bijou Theater in town. No more movies for me. Good-bye, World!

I stood by the desk until the library emptied, and Miss Evans closed the door. I thought I was going to faint. I had never fainted, but was positive today would be the day for that experience. I panicked as she walked over to me. I would say nothing. Wasn't there some Constitutional Amendment I could claim to protect me? I waited for her to speak.

"Anne, I am glad to talk to you. I've noticed you are here most days and Saturdays. You are one of the library's most consistent users, and I'd like to thank you for that. If people don't use the library, all these books would go to waste, and then I wouldn't have this job, so thank you."

I wasn't sure where this was going, and since I didn't have a voice anyway, I just nodded.

"Tell me about your reading. What books are you favorites? Do you like a particular author or type of book? How many books a week do you read? And explain why you hide the book you read when you are in here."

I took a deep breath and answered her questions. I liked to read all kinds of books. Currently I was reading Edgar Allan Poe stories although I couldn't understand all the words he used and had to look them up in our *Webster's Dictionary*. I could only take two books out a week from the library and usually read them twice because I was a fast reader and finished them in a few days. When I had nothing else to read at home, I would read through the dictionary and the atlas we had. I regularly reread all the books in our small home library. I read the *Bible* but I did not really like it. I was not able to take out books that were labeled *Adult* until I was twelve, and I was still eleven, so I read them while in the library. I hid them so I could finish them, and I was sorry if I broke any rules, but I did not know about them and did not mean to.

I took a deep breath. No fainting yet. No Sheriff Samms yet. No throwing me out of the library by the seat of my pants, just like in the Three Stooges movie Josh and I saw once at the Bijou. At least not yet. Miss Evans listened, and then she nodded when I finished.

"Well, you seem to be quite a *voracious* reader. Do you know what that word means?"

I shook my head.

"It means a person who is an *avid* reader, one who is *ravenous* for books and loves to read. Does that describe you?"

"Yes, Ma'am, I think it does." I was not quite sure about the other words she had used, but was not going to disagree at this point.

"That's a good thing, you know. I understand that, and since I am in charge here, I think we can make some changes to the rules. Please go and get the book you hid, and bring it to me."

I went to the very back of the stacks and reached under the pile of books and pulled out Willa Cather's *O Pioneers!* and brought it to her. I handed her the novel and waited for the sentence to be pronounced. Miss Evans looked at it and then smiled.

"Do you like this book? Is it a good story?" she asked.

"I do, but some of it is hard to read. I think the author might use too many words. But I'm almost finished with it. Emil just got shot, and I don't know what happened then. Honestly, once I found your note, I couldn't read today."

Miss Evans took the book and went behind her desk. She filled out a paper and then stamped the book. She looked at me and spoke.

"The most important question to ask about a book is: *Does it tell a good story*? If you can answer in the affirmative, then your time has not been wasted. This applies to both fiction and non-fiction. A good story is the first rule."

Ruth Evans came around the desk and stopped in front of me. She handed me the Cather book.

"It would be a shame not to find out what happens, and it's a long time until Monday after school. I signed this out to you so you can take it home and finish it over the weekend. When you return it, see me. There are two more books that come after this one. I'll have the second book of the trilogy here for you. It's called *The Song of the Lark*. There is a third book, but this library doesn't own it yet. That title is *My Antonia*, and I'm going to order it Monday."

I took the book and placed it on top of the other two I held. I stared at this woman who had just broken the library rules. Perhaps *she* would be arrested.

"But this is an adult book, and I already have two books signed out to me. Is this going to be O.K.?"

"Yes, Anne, this is fine. I will make a deal with you. I can allow you to continue your library reading while here, but don't hide the book. Just hand it to me, and I will place it behind the main desk for safekeeping. Also, since you are almost twelve, I'm going to allow you to take books from the *Adult Section,* and I will increase the number you can take out at one time to three. And when you finish those three, bring them back, even if the week is not up, and you may take three more. How does that sound?"

I was astonished. I was delighted. I was not going to jail!

"Thank you, Miss Evans! I really appreciate it, and I will be careful with all the books. And if there is something you want me to do, I can do it."

"Since you are here almost daily, would you mind if I asked you to sometimes shelve books? I can teach you how to do that. You would be a great help to me, sort of an assistant librarian."

I took a deep breath, "I'll be glad to."

"And if every now and then I gave you a book to read while in the library, would you take my suggestion and read it? We might even talk about it when you are finished."

"Sure, that would be great. I don't have anyone to really talk about the stuff I read."

"Then we should shake on our agreement, Anne. And then you should be getting home. I know you want to find out about Emil. I'll see you on Monday."

We shook hands sealing the deal. I had never shaken a hand before. Another first. I smiled at Miss Evans, and as she smiled back at me, I thought her smile made her look pretty, and her eyes were the greenest I had ever seen.

I left the library and headed home clutching my three books, including the one from the *Adult Section*. I felt like a real grown-up. As I walked back to our farm, I thought about my morning. I wondered about this new librarian who had, with a few marks on a paper, changed my world. Her authority had opened the realm of books to me in a way it had never been before. I was looking forward to Monday and to returning my three books and getting three more. And beginning my new job. I was important. I was now Miss Evan's assistant librarian.

Miss Evan's Assistant Librarian

The years of seventh, eighth, and ninth grades were filled with so much reading that my mother threatened to keep me at home if I didn't pay more attention to my chores. I think she was joking because she took some of the library books I brought home and read them during her Sunday reading times. Once she came into the library with me on a Saturday, early in my assistantship, to meet Ruth Evans. They spoke for a while, and then Mother left, but before she did, she smiled and nodded at me. I assumed that meant my spending so much time at the library met with her approval. At least she never said anything else about it as long as I kept up with my chores and school grades. And I made sure to do that.

For the first few months, Ruth allowed me to choose my own library reading from the stacks. And all the stacks were open for my use. Once, during that first year, when I handed her my special book to keep behind the main desk, she took it and said, "Anne, when you finish this one, I have a book for you to read. Let me know when you are ready for it."

I nodded my head. When I completed my chosen book, I went to her to get my assigned reading, and she handed me a copy of Dicken's *Oliver Twist*. I thought she just wanted me to read it, but Ruth gave me an additional assignment.

"As you read this, I want you to think about good and evil. Decide who is good in the book and who is evil. And consider why they are that way. This book should be easy for you, and that is why I want to start with it. The next one will be more challenging. When you finish it, we can figure out some time to discuss it."

I read the book, and I thought about what Miss Evans asked me to consider. When the time came for us to talk about it, I was surprised. Ruth asked me to stay later, one Saturday, and once we straightened up and closed the library, she telephoned my mother to ask permission for me to stay longer. Then, she and I walked the few streets over to the house where she was living with her uncle, Doctor Evans, and we had lunch at the kitchen table while we talked about Dicken's novel. That first time, I was not sure what to expect and was subdued in my answers and unsure in the discussion, but she made me feel so at ease that my difficulty did not last. After our discussion, she handed me the next book which was Dostoevsky's *Crime and Punishment*.

"This reading will challenge you," explained Ruth, "and I am going to ask you the same question: who is good and who is evil, and why? Read with that purpose in mind."

And that is how the assignments began. With *good and evil* as my guiding purpose, I read through Stevenson's *Dr. Jekyll and Mr. Hyde,* Melville's *Moby Dick,* and his *Billy Budd.* The discussions we had were always challenging, but I soon learned to support my thoughts and beliefs, and after the first five assigned books, Ruth changed the theme. We discussed *changes* through these novels: Cather's *My Antonia* (Ruth had ordered the book as she promised), Dreiser's *Sister Carrie,* London's *The Call of the Wild,* and Hugo's *Les Misérables.* The Hugo book took me a longer time to read than even *Moby Dick,* and I had never read anything that complicated with so many characters, but I got through it. And always, Ruth would ask after each book: *Was this a good story?*

When we completed the discussion about changes, Ruth asked me a question I was not prepared for. She wanted to know if a *change* could be *good* or *evil.* I did not know how to answer, and said nothing.

"Well, why don't you consider that question over this next week? We can talk about it again."

And we did. And through the years, up through my high school graduation and beyond, Ruth Evans taught me in this way. She guided my reading, and challenged my thinking. I read about religions and slavery and morality and ethics and love and honor and greed, and we branched out to the ancient philosophers and medieval texts that were in Harrison Greenwood's old collection. Although I was never able to attend college, I did not mind because I believed Ruth gave me an exceptional liberal arts education.

She also taught me how to work in the library, starting with shelving the books. Soon I was managing the front desk and organizing the card catalogue. I watched the process as she ordered additional materials and repaired torn books, and when she was sure I could take over those tasks, she gave them to me. As money became available (and Ruth was continually going to the various civic organizations' meetings and somehow obtaining funds from them), she expanded the Research Section of the library with a new set of *Funk and Wagnall's Encyclopedia,* various dictionaries, and a myriad of reference materials I had never heard of or seen before. Then she showed me how to use all the materials and set me tasks to look up various answers, so I would be able help other students find information for their school assignments.

This was a lengthy process and did not happen quickly. I improved at my assigned tasks and became absorbed in the work at the library. The first years I worked as a volunteer, but when I entered tenth grade, Ruth went to the newly formed Library Board's meeting and insisted that I be paid for my hours and work at the library. The money was minimal, but I was proud to be earning it and brought it home to share with my parents. The times were difficult, and everyone was doing the best they could with the little they had. My family was no different.

I was being groomed to work in the library, and I knew that and was pleased. Ruth and I became friends, and when we were alone, addressed each other by our first, familiar names. Once when we were cleaning up on a Saturday afternoon, I asked her why she had decided I would be her "special project".

"*Special project?*" and Ruth looked at me and laughed. "I am not sure what you mean, but, Anne, I looked at you and it was like looking in a mirror at myself at your age. Your family situation is different than mine was. I argued with my parents, especially my father who believes females are inferior to males and do not need an education. That I was able to work and finagle my way through two years of college is still astounding to me. When I returned home, I was pushed and cajoled and brow-beaten and was expected to marry our neighbor, a widowed farmer, who was looking for a woman to raise his four children. That was not going to happen, and I spent years quarreling with my parents, especially my father. When Uncle Emmanuel offered to open his house to me, I jumped at the chance to leave." She stopped here and stared off into space.

"And now, I have said too much. But we have become friends, and you are more sophisticated than your years, and now you know something of my past. I just wanted to make things easier for you. You have an intelligence I noted, and a great imagination, and I wanted to help, and frankly, I enjoy our talks. And that is enough. There, Miss Assistant, those books still need to be shelved."

I went to the books on the table and gathered them up. Then I turned and asked another question that was certainly none of my business.

"Ruth, did you ever want to marry? I don't mean that old widowed farmer, but what if someone came along? What then?"

Ruth smiled. Then she laughed.

"I don't see that happening, Anne. Not that I have anything against marriage; it's a fine institution and one I admire. But in this small town? No, Anne, I have met no man I want to marry or who wants to marry me. And I am happy with this career, my career. Now let's get this work done. I promised Uncle Emmanuel I would bake his favorite cinnamon cake for tonight."

We finished our work and then locked up the building. I turned to go home to the farm, and Ruth walked to her house to complete her baking. We parted ways, and I took a few steps before I turned around to watch the tall, thin woman stride down the walk, greeting the townspeople she passed, periodically stopping to talk briefly or answer a question. Her brown hair was pulled back at the nape of her neck with one stubborn lock that fell into her face, and her heels clicked along the pavement. I listened to them fade as I turned and proceeded down Smokehouse Road to my home.

Later, several years later, I remembered our conversation, and wondered about it. I considered destiny. I speculated about fate. We don't know what is in store for us, I decided. Perhaps the Ancients were correct: no matter our individual determinations, the stars would rule. I thought this was the case because despite her certitude about future matrimonial prospects, Ruth Evans ended up getting married. And she married the most handsome and eligible man anyone in the town of Everstille had ever seen. She married Tobias Pinkerton.

Tobias Pinkerton

The Pinkertons, Samuel and Ethel, lived in the house down the road from our farm. Their daughters were older than my brothers although their son, Tobias, was about the same age as Davie. I never knew them well because I was young when Samuel Pinkerton died and Ethel took her children, Gladys and Tobias, and moved to Chicago to live with her older daughter, Ernestine, and her husband, Amos. Tobias finished growing up in that city, attended college, became a teacher, and worked there before returning to the place he was born. Before returning to Everstille and teaching in the high school. Before becoming the most eligible bachelor and the handsomest man to ever live in our town. And that opinion was not just mine.

A description of Tobias would not do him justice. I could say that his height was six feet, two inches, and his shoulders were broad and muscular under his coat, earned by his swimming and general physical activity. I might try to capture the color of his hair which I have heard others call *flaxen*, or *golden*, or even *gilded*, and expound on the thickness of it as it curled along his nape when he needed a haircut, and the way one untamed curl flopped into his face and caressed the thick medium brown eyebrows even as he continually pushed it back, trying to force it into place. Under those eyebrows and the teeming lashes were his eyes which, if I had ever seen the blue Aegean Sea, I might describe as bluer than the Aegean Sea. How to describe the shape of his cheekbones? Perhaps they could be christened *softly jagged*, an oxymoron that fails mightily. I heard some girls once call his square jaw *meaningfully well-defined*, and while I don't think they knew what they meant and were just playing with words, they were right. When he smiled there were sparkling white teeth which showed, and a small clef kissed his manly chin. But none of these accounts, no word pictures, none of the lofty narratives can account for the substantial fineness of Tobias Pinkerton. I will wait for a new language to be developed before attempting to portray him.

Add to that, he was kind. And generous, humane, considerate, charitable, thoughtful, seriously intelligent, and amusing. That I was fifteen, and he taught the high school English class I was lucky enough to be assigned to had, I am sure, nothing to do with my feelings. Or any of the other fifteen or sixteen or seventeen-year-old girls who were not assigned to any of his classes but created a steady line to the assistant principal's office attempting to be transferred into his class. Any of the classes he taught. Those senior girls who were eighteen, fantasized a wedding scene in which Mr. Pinkerton played the groom who waited in eager anticipation at the altar for them. Even those senior girls who were planning real weddings, and who had suddenly become left-handed to show off their diminutive engagement rings, compared their intended grooms with the English teacher, and the smiles they had maintained since their engagements took on a slightly discontented edge. The high school males found admiration in his physique which they noted because he coached the swim team. Thus, Tobias Pinkerton had returned to Everstille to become the most popular teacher at the high school.

When the news of his teaching job broke during the end of summer, and Tobias was seen driving his fully packed car into the town and moving into one of the small rental apartments on Charming Lane (Yes, that was the name. Someone on Everstille's Town Council had a sense of humor.), a coterie of women who had daughters of marriageable age brought casseroles, cakes, and Jell-O molds to his apartment as welcome offerings. Or possible bribes. In all cases, it was carefully explained to him, their daughters were the ones who had whipped up, without any problem and certainly no help from their mother, these masterpieces of culinary expertise. Poor Tobias. His digestive system must have felt the affronts of the victuals for weeks.

I wanted to know about this person who was shaking up our town, so I rode my old bicycle to my brother Davie's place to ask about him. I knew that he and Ray had known the family and gone to school with Tobias before the Pinkertons had moved. I found both my brothers at Davie's house sitting on the porch, just finished with the day's chores, and planning the following day's tasks.

"Hello, little sister," and Davie waved to me. "Haven't seen you in a while. Are you still haunting the library and eating up those books?"

"Yes, I am. Hi, Ray. How are things?"

"Fine, kiddo. What brings you to these parts?" Ray took a long drink of the lemonade in his hand and then reached over to pour another glass and held it out to me.

"No, thanks. Have you heard about the new English teacher at the school? You two know him."

Davie shook his head. "We don't always get the news very quickly out here. Who is it?"

"It's Tobias Pinkerton from the Pinkerton family who used to live down Smokehouse Road from us. You went to school with him, right?"

Davie put his lemonade down and looked at me. Then he and Ray looked at each other. I wasn't sure what those looks meant, but there was something there, and I didn't understand it.

Davie answered. "We did, but that was a long time ago. So, he's a teacher? He would be about my age, I guess. What have you heard?"

"I haven't heard anything. Except I will be in his English class this fall. I thought you could tell me something about him. You should hear all the girls talk. Half of the town already has him married off to someone. What was he like? Do you remember? Was he always as good-looking as he is now? What can you tell me?"

Ray gave some sort of snort, and Davie threw him a look that I caught but could not interpret. Davie picked up his glass and drank the rest of the liquid. He looked at me and said:

"There's not much I can tell you. That was a long time ago, and we were just starting high school when old Mr. Pinkerton died and the family moved. Even though we grew up next to each other, Toby wasn't close friends to Ray and me. Didn't spend much time with him. He was considered smart and stayed to himself most of the time, so sorry, Anne, I can't tell you much more than that. So, he's good-looking according to the town?"

"He was always pretty," said Ray and gave a side-long glance to Davie who looked at him and slightly shook his head. "I mean hand-some," and Ray looked down at his shoes. They were both quiet and did not look at each other

There was something I was not catching here, but I knew my brothers. It was obvious they had become clams. I would not be privy to whatever knowledge about Tobias they had, if they, in fact, had any information. This I knew.

Finally, Davie looked over to me. "Well, all I can say is, hand-some or not, he's your teacher, so you'll need to do your work and behave."

"Davie, you know I always do. And will. Well, that's the news I have, and I better get back for supper. Bye. See you two later, I guess."

I turned my bicycle around and started home. Davie and Ray yelled their good-byes to me, and I rode off. I turned around and glanced back to see them standing and talking animatedly to each other. Whatever they knew about Tobias, I guess I wouldn't be told the information. Possibly there was nothing special to know.

As I rode home, I thought about things. Maybe Tobias Pinkerton was just another teacher who gave out boring assignments and stupid pop quizzes. Maybe his softly-jagged cheekbones and meaningfully well-defined jaw and blue Aegean Sea eyes were just a facade that hid a typical uninspiring educator. Maybe that manly chin hid the fact that his class would be as boring as other classes I had taken. I supposed I would find out soon enough. Whatever he was, he could never be as interesting and as informative a teacher as Ruth Evans. She was someone who stood well above whatever his abilities might prove to be. She was someone who would remain the best teacher in my life. I am sure he could never match her. I doubt they would ever cross paths. They could never, ever, I was positive, even be friends.

Friends

I was wrong. Tobias Pinkerton and Ruth Evans became friends. Tobias was a resourceful teacher and was unafraid to attempt innovative assignments. His English classes were given projects and essays which needed support and required research. I had no problem doing this because of the training Ruth had given me over the years, but there were several students who had no idea what was required, had never actually been to the Greenwood Library, and were, in fact, unsure exactly where it was. No other teacher had ever given tasks like this, and once Tobias realized that this was not just a new type of assignment, but that the majority of his students would need to be walked through this, baby step by baby step, he went to the library, talked to Ruth about what he wanted his students to do and enlisted her help. This was the start of their friendship.

Tobias and Ruth did something unusual for the time. They worked together. They connected the public school and the public library. They showed the students that the library was not just a housing for dusty old books, but contained actual information. Relevant, timely, important information. Ruth worked with Tobias and the two of them taught his classes how to search for facts, find pertinent information, and use it to write their papers. The final papers were not good. And the second assignment wasn't much better. But, by the third paper, about half of the students caught on to the process, and Tobias was pleased. So pleased, that he asked Ruth, as a thank you, to have a dinner with him at Mazie's, where they both had the Wednesday Blue-Plate Special and a good time.

At first, I was jealous. I was unsure of exactly who I had the jealous feelings about. Certainly, I was jealous of Ruth. She got to spend time with Tobias, looking at those softly jagged cheekbones and staring into those blue Aegean Sea eyes. I was equally jealous of Tobias who got to spend time with Ruth. My Ruth. He would talk with her, and ask her questions, and listen to her wonderful, clear, and controlled answers. I was sure "Mazie Meetings" would not become a habit. They did.

I got over it. From what I could see, this was simply a friendship, and when I was honest with myself, I admitted that Ruth needed a friend who was not fifteen years old. She spent so much time at the library that there was little time for her to form female friendships. Besides, there were few females in Everstille who were her age and single. By the time Everstille women were as old as Ruth, they were married and had children to watch and a house to care for, and a few of them had part-time jobs to help bolster their husband's pay-checks There was little time for friendships. Especially with unmarried, childless women.

The same applied to Tobias although being a male, he did have freedoms females did not. He was free to visit places like Mazie's for a solitary meal, or join various male teachers for a card game, or travel to South Bend for a minor league baseball outing. But there was no one to discuss the important ideas he found so stimulating. No one to discuss and deliberate about religions and slavery and morality and ethics and love and honor and greed and good and evil as they applied to literature and life. His male colleagues wanted to enjoy activities like card games and baseball outings, and would rather leave literature and history and thematic discussions to the classroom. So, there formed a connection between Tobias and Ruth which had started in the library and continued at Mazie's every Wednesday when the Blue-Plate Special was offered and profound conversation was appreciated.

The town noticed the friendship, and, to the distress of many of the mothers with daughters of marriageable age, a wedding was expected. This probability was discussed at length. I heard the whispers in the school hallways, and at meetings of the Women's Auxiliary to the Civic Council at Large (W.A.C.C.) held in a library's meeting room, and especially at church, before the service started and after the service ended. It was a shame that such an available and handsome man, such a true gentleman and intellect would end up with Miss Plain Jane. Certainly, Ruth Evans was smart. After all she did get that library job, and does keep the place organized and clean, and did complete two years of college. But, the two of them together? Shocking! Besides, Ruth was older than Tobias, but by how much? Three years? Four years? There could not be any children, could there be? The discussions and the possibilities about the ruination of these two lives was fodder for dialogue for months. And then the months turned into years. And then, as their relationship became accepted and established, discussions decreased.

Ruth and Tobias remained friends. They were seen at the school dances as chaperones, at swim meets where Tobias coached the swim team, at the Methodist Episcopal Church services where they sat together and walked home together afterwards, at the Christmas party given by the combined Everstille Civic Organizations (E.C.O.), at all the yearly parades and festivals and events. They did not hold hands or touch in any unsuitable way, but, as a gentleman would, Tobias took Ruth's arm when they crossed the street, and helped her up the steps or curb. What was noticed was Tobias' disinterest in seeing any other woman socially. A few forward young women asked him to accompany them to various concerts, or parties, or social events, and he was so genuinely tender and considerate when turning them down that they walked away believing they might still have a chance with him; that at some point, there would be an affirmative answer to their invitation; that just looking at his meaningfully defined jaw and blue Aegean Sea eyes as he refused their invitations was, in fact, enough. Years passed, and acceptance about the indisputably platonic friendship of Ruth Evans and Tobias Pinkerton set in.

I must admit, I wondered about it myself. I was prone to periodically asking inappropriate questions of Ruth, but she let me know when I crossed that line. I watched them together and saw nothing but friendship between them. Once I became a high school graduate and was hired to work full-time at the library, I was sometimes included in their discussions about a book we had all read, but I was never invited to join them at Mazie's for the Wednesday evening specials or sit with them at church where they shared a hymnal and harmonized to *The Church's One Foundation.* Duets, yes; trios, no. Or, so I thought.

They kept up a friendship which peripherally included me. That I did not mind was because of Tobias' travels. About every month, he would leave Everstille on a Friday night and travel to Chicago for the weekend to see his family. At least that is what Ruth explained to me when I questioned her. During the school's summer breaks, Tobias would be gone for longer periods, perhaps weeks. Ruth said he was updating his teaching skills at various seminars, and taking classes towards another degree, and that all made sense to me. But when Toby was absent, she seemed dejected and glum, and I noticed her daydreaming while she sat in her office, something I never detected before the arrival of the blue Aegean Sea eyes.

However, I was glad for these weekend trips. Ruth and I would fall back into our habit of a Saturday lunch and book discussion. She no longer assigned me reading, but would take suggestions from me about the books we discussed. Over the years, I acquired the job of ordering additional books, and that was a task I took seriously. I read book reviews and took periodic trips in my Dad's old truck to Elkhart and even to South Bend where I spoke to the librarians at the larger libraries there and asked for their input. I would scrutinize their *New Book* section, skim through the texts, take notes, and make decisions for our own library.

Few books were ordered during the war years due to financial cutbacks in all areas, but once the war ended, and the town expanded and the citizens began to demand their money's worth of public services, the library budget increased. As did our salaries. I was delighted with that because then I could afford to purchase a used car, and there is nothing that makes one feel more grown up than having to pay for your own gas, oil, and upkeep. There was even talk at City Council meetings of expanding the library because our holdings were increasing, and we were getting crowded. The two meeting rooms at the back of the library were used for all the civic organization meetings including the new Boy Scout group that was started, and the spaces were in constant demand. The library was turning out to be one of the most popular places in town. There was no doubt that Ruth Evans was responsible for the public's increasing regard for the Harrison Greenwood Public Library.

I remained busy and happy there. I did things occasionally with some friends, including Harold, one of the boys I had known since elementary school. We often went to events together. There was nothing romantic about our relationship, and I saw Harold as a friend which allowed me to better understand the bond between Ruth and Tobias.

I still lived at home with my parents who were aging and pondering what to do with the farm. They were considering selling at least part of it, and possibly all of it, to The Goodwin Construction and Building Company. The corporation was buying farms in the surrounding area, clearing the land, and readying it for new houses. My older siblings had moved away, and the only one to help Dad was Josh, who had built a place close to the old farmhouse. I knew that eventually I would need to look for somewhere to live on my own in the main town which was expanding and growing. New families were spreading out in the area, and most of the new citizens came to town on a regular basis to use the library. Life in Everstille was transforming and shifting, and I felt part of it.

Tobias was part of the change. Just after the war ended, Everstille High School's Principal Jenkins retired, and Tobias Pinkerton was offered the job. He was young to have such an important position, being in his early thirties, but his popularity, inventive teaching techniques, and proven ability to manage large classes pushed him to the forefront of a very short list. And he was willing to take on much more responsibility for very little additional remuneration. Personally, I think those blue Aegean Sea eyes may have swayed Mrs. Hoffsteader who was the female portion of the School Board.

He discussed this offer with Ruth who encouraged him to take it. No one else could do the job as well, and all those ideas he had for improving the school could be employed. He was the most logical person for the job with his innovative notions and modern concepts about education. I know Ruth said this to him because I was standing right outside the empty meeting room after the School Board left, and I was eavesdropping as the two of them talked. A bad habit, I know. And I did try to look surprised when they came up to the Circulation Desk where I had hurriedly placed myself and told me the exciting news…Tobias Pinkerton, teacher, was soon to be Tobias Pinkerton, principal.

Tobias Pinkerton, Principal

Tobias Pinkerton moved seamlessly from the position of *Teacher* to that of *Principal.* There was no discernible faculty professional jealousy as he went from being a classroom colleague to a building administrator. Well, except for Jim (Jimbo) Reynolds, the football coach and freshman math teacher, who was the other candidate on the short list for the position. Jim Reynolds was married; he and his overwrought wife, Marianne had a brood of five children, and even the small bump in pay would have been helpful in fitting the growing group with shoes and paying for the music lessons Marianne insisted their three daughters take. But it was not to be. While, outwardly, Jimbo pretended to be relieved he was not the chosen one, inwardly, he was upset. He was, however, the first to shake Tobias' hand enthusiastically and proclaim congratulations loudly. But he and Marianne groused at home about the lost opportunity and the continued difficulties in paying for the music lessons.

"I just think, Jim, that it is strange someone in Tobias' position and his age is not married. I wonder…Jennie, Stop that!...why not? After all, he is considered a catch. By some, that is."

"Not sure, Hon. But he is almost as old as me, and he has had chances, I am sure. Guess some men aren't meant to be married," and Jimbo took a second to remember, fondly, his own bachelor days as his second-oldest daughter began to practice *Fur Elise* on the piano. Again. For the umpteenth time.

"Just strange. I was talking about it with some of the women at church, and he has refused to go to dinner twice with Gwen Rutherford's daughter. And her daughter is quite a looker. Don't you think?"

Jimbo wasn't sure exactly who Gwen Rutherford's daughter was or what she looked like, but he shrugged and grunted assent. "Yes, but, again, maybe Pinkerton isn't the marrying kind. After all, your Uncle Milton isn't married."

Marianne looked around to make sure there were no little ears in the vicinity before she raised her eyebrows and leaned in to mutter, "And you know why, don't you?"

Jimbo turned to look at his wife. His look was a startled one, a considered one, a thoughtful one. "Hmmm…" he answered.

Now I am unsure this was the exact way the dialogue went, but as I sat in church before Sunday services, two pews behind Marianne

Reynolds, I did hear her report this conversation rather loudly to Patricia Jones who sat in the pew directly in front of me. I composed the imagined exchange in my mind as I gazed attentively at my hymnal. I admit continuing my eavesdropping habit. This exchange was upsetting. And puzzling.

I was unsure exactly who Marianne's Uncle Milton was or why he had never married or exactly what was implied by the conversation. But I remembered the comments my brothers made years ago, and the implication that there was more than they were willing to tell me, and I was putting together bits of gossip and rumors which mentioned Tobias. A picture was beginning to form. I concede my naiveté in matters of the heart. I had grown up on a farm and understood the workings of animal physicality and had read enough to know about human love and body carnality, but I had no experience with it myself. I suspected what the women were talking about was most likely not fit material for discussion in the House of God, and I determined to do some research at the library for myself. I needed to understand what was being implied about Tobias.

After services, I told my parents I needed to do some important work at the library, and they should not wait Sunday dinner for me. I would eat later. I drove to Greenwood Library and parked the car. Using my key, I let myself in and relocked the door behind me, but the light was on, and I was surprised to find Ruth there. She had not been in church, but this was a weekend Tobias was gone on a family visit to Chicago, so while I was not surprised she wasn't there, I was taken aback to see her here.

"Hello, Ruth. I didn't see you in church and thought you were at home. Is there a problem or something I can help you do?"

"Hello, Anne. No, no church for me this morning. I'm going to take a couple days off this week so I can help Uncle Emmanuel with some of his packing, and I came here to finish up some orders that need to be sent out. I was going to call you later and let you know. Uncle Emmanuel has been invited to a farewell lunch and later a supper, so he isn't available to do any packing or sorting today. Why are you here?"

Doctor Evans was retiring and going to live with his sister, and his house was going to be sold. I knew Ruth was looking for another place to live, and she currently was busy with several personal decisions, and I was not sure whether I should upset her with the conversation I heard or any questions I might have. Anyway, it was just gossip. And what exactly was I going to research anyway? What was I looking for?

"I thought I left my umbrella here so I was going to check. It might rain tomorrow. But, since I'm here, we can go over what you want me to take care of while you're gone a few days. Guess it's a good thing I stopped."

I went to the main desk and opened the drawer assigned to me for my personal effects, and looked through it. I knew there was no umbrella there. It was home in my bedroom on the floor of my closet where I had left it, but I gave everything a good look, moved things around, then shrugged my shoulders. Add lying to my list of sins.

"No, it's not here. I guess I left it somewhere else. I'll have to look more carefully at home. Well, since I'm here, let's go over what you want to happen the next few days."

We pulled chairs together, and Ruth outlined the orders and a few other secretarial items she would normally have done herself. There was nothing with which I needed much guidance, but I asked some questions and attempted to keep her talking while I tried to decide whether I should say anything. We organized the materials for Monday's work and together shelved some books. Ruth seemed to be unusually quiet. I asked a few unimportant questions as we finished the tasks, and when I looked at her, I decided she needed company.

"Ruth, Mother has Sunday dinner made, and I told her I would eat when I got home. Why don't you come with me and have some? You could spend the afternoon, and I'll drive you home later. We haven't talked books for a while, and it might be a good outing for you."

Ruth looked at me and said, "Thanks, Anne. I think I would like that. I don't want to spend the afternoon by myself today. Are you sure I won't be a bother?"

"Not a bit. Mother always makes a big Sunday dinner because some of the family often stops over later. She'll be happy to see you. Let me just telephone and let her know we're coming."

We left the library and walked to my car. As I drove to the farm, I kept up a running conversation. Ruth didn't speak much and seemed preoccupied, but I continued to chatter. Dad greeted us as we came into the house, and Mother moved us into the large kitchen where the table was set for two. She served the meal and told Ruth how glad she was to see her, and if anything was needed, Ruth should be sure to ask me. Then she excused herself for her Sunday reading time.

Ruth and I busied ourselves eating for a few minutes. I asked her if she had completed Huxley's *Brave New World* yet and wanted to talk about it. Ruth took another bite of the mashed potatoes and a sip of water before she answered.

"Not yet, Anne. I haven't had a chance to read much with all the moving and packing and trying to decide on where I am going to live. Uncle Emmanuel is still looking for a buyer for the house, but when he leaves in a month, I will need to have a place to move. If I could buy his house, I would, but that's not possible. Anyway, about the book: what I have read so far is fascinating, but I'm not ready to discuss it yet. I think Toby is almost done with it, so maybe the three of us can talk about it in a few weeks. Sorry. I know you were looking forward to a discussion."

"That's fine, Ruth. Speaking of him, how is Toby finding the principal business?"

Ruth was again quiet and took a few extra chews before answering, "He likes it."

That was all she said. We finished eating, and I pushed my plate to the side. There was something wrong, and I did not know what it was. This entire day had disturbed me. In fact, I realized that I had been disturbed for weeks. I stood and picked up our plates and moved them to the sink area. I looked around and saw the cherry crumble Mother had made.

"Oh, there is cherry crumble, Ruth. How about a dish?"

"Sounds great, but maybe later. Let's do up the dishes so your mother does not need to. It's the least I can do for such a great meal. And then, why don't we go for a walk? Maybe we can walk down the old part of Smokehouse Road you told me about and see where your great-uncles lived. I just feel like getting out in the fresh air for a while."

We did exactly that after stopping to thank Mother for the food and telling her we were going for a walk. She nodded and waved us off as she continued to read her book. The afternoon was pleasant for early spring. No rain clouds in sight, and the path was dry. I pointed the way, and as we strolled down the path, I indicated to Ruth where the Martin cows used to graze, and showed her the tree I would sit in to read. The farm and the cows were both gone, slowly being replaced by new houses and families. As we neared the area where the old shack used to be, we noted a few rotted planks on the ground; weeds, and moss, and a few early blooming pinks were covering the area. Nature was reclaiming her space. We stood and looked around, feeling the chill come through the still bare oak limbs, and even the sun that came through did not bring enough warmth.

"My parents are thinking about selling at least this part of their land. The farm is too much for them, and they are going to need to do something with it. My brother Josh helps, but his family is growing, and he says he needs to get a different job that pays, so I suspect in the next couple of years there will be changes. In fact, Mother and Dad are considering eventually moving into town, although I'm not so sure they will be happy in such a small confined area after spending their lives out here."

Ruth listened as she looked around at the place. "Probably two or three houses could fit in here if some of those trees were taken down. They are old and lovely, and it will be a shame to lose them. But I guess that's the price of progress."

We stood silently. Then I decided to ask the question that had been bothering me. Ruth could answer it or not.

"Ruth, what's the matter? You are not the same, and honestly, I have a feeling it has more to do with Tobias than with your uncle's move and your need to find a new place to stay. If this is none of my business, then, tell me. I won't ask again."

When Ruth looked up at me, wet shadows blurred her green eyes. She wiped them away with the corner of her sweater, took a deep breath, and let it out with a quiet sigh. I was shocked. I had seen Ruth in many moods, but I had never seen her weepy.

"Toby has asked me to marry him."

"That's wonderful! Why would that make you upset?"

Ruth looked down at the ground and pushed some brown leaves away with her foot. She was considering whether to tell me or not. I knew this, and as much as I wanted to know her secret, I would accept whatever she decided to do. If she did not tell me, I would not ask again. If she did, I would keep her secret.

"Anne, Toby and I have discussed this at length. There are things I can't tell you although you might guess. However, don't make this into a game because I won't play. If I agree to marry him, it will be a marriage in name only. We will live together, but we won't live *together*, and I won't explain more than that. I know there have been rumors and gossip, and both of us have ignored them, but to stop them, and so he can continue to work at being principal, a marriage seems essential. It would be advantageous for me too, I guess. I told him I would have an answer for him when we meet at Mazie's next Wednesday. That's the real reason

I am taking some time off. I'll help with uncle's packing and sorting, but I need some time to be alone and think. Obviously, I am asking for your word about never saying anything."

"Ruth, I won't say a thing. And whatever you decide will be the right decision. I do have one other question, and you don't need to answer it. Is there any love in this relationship? Do you love Tobias? Does he love you? I think if that is the case, things might work out in the future."

"I think we both love each other, but it's not romantic, not a husband and wife love. We are friends, and we trust each other. He has confided in me. I know his secrets as he knows mine. Toby is reliable and intelligent and caring. But things will not change. And, Anne, that is all I will say."

"Alright, Ruth; I understand. Thanks for trusting me. I hope you know that I want the best for you and Tobias. And, I'll keep my mouth shut."

She came over to me and hugged me. This was a first. She smiled, and we began walking back to the farm. Nothing else was said about her decision, and when we got home, Josh and his family were there. We all had cherry crumble and talked, and laughed, and watched Josh's young children play, and then I drove her back to her uncle's house. I meant what I promised Ruth. I have never said anything. Until now. *Promise-breaking*. A longer list of sins.

***

The following Thursday when I came into the library, Ruth was there in her small office. I hung up my coat and placed my things in the drawer. It was early, and we would not officially open for about twenty minutes. I looked at the pile of paperwork Ruth had placed on the desk for me and began to sift through it. After about ten minutes, I looked towards the office and waved to Ruth who waved back. She walked out of her office, past the back stacks, and came to stand in front of me. Smiling, she took my hand and held it as she asked if I would be the maid-of-honor for their wedding.

Their Wedding

Mason Chessworth, owner, and editor of the *The Everstille News*, a six-page, bi-weekly local newspaper, wrote a glowing story about the newly married couple whose headline proclaimed: "Head of the High School and Head of the Library Marry Proving Two Heads Are Better Than One". Mason Chessworth prided himself on his wit and ability to arrange words in a pleasing manner. He mostly pleased himself and his wife, Francine. The headline was followed by a rather lengthy article about the wedding which was surprising because Mason Chessworth was not at the nuptials. The wedding was a small event at the Methodist Episcopal Church with only family and very few friends in attendance.

Ruth Evans and Tobias Pinkerton were wed on the Saturday before the week of Spring Break. Ruth's uncle, Doctor Evans was there, and her parents came with one of her sisters. Tobias' mother and his youngest sister, Gladys, were there. A few teachers from the high school were invited, as were my parents because I stood up with Ruth. There was nothing fancy about the ceremony, the wedding attire, or the simple cake and coffee reception held afterwards in the church's Reception Hall. Everyone was pleased to see Ruth and Tobias married, and by three o'clock, the festivities were over, everyone had wished the newly married couple well, and the guests were on their way home.

Ruth's family hugged her and shook Tobias' hand, and Tobias' mother and sister hugged them both before leaving. Doctor Evans did not stay because he was traveling to his sister's where he was going to spend his retirement, and his car was loaded and ready to go. Most of his personal belongings had been sent ahead, while much of the furniture was being left with the house which had been sold to Ruth and Tobias. Together, they would be able to afford it, and Ruth was delighted. I was too because I was going to be able to move into Tobias' apartment on Charming Lane. The three of us were going to spend the week moving furniture, cleaning, and setting up our new homes. No honeymoon was scheduled.

By mid-week, the moving was done. Ruth and I agreed to work alternate days at the library because someone needed to be there to supervise, but Tobias had the week off, and with the help of a couple of other coaches, moved and arranged the heavy furniture. I transported my bedroom set and an old kitchen table and two chairs that had been stored in the barn, in my Dad's truck, and once they were in place, began cleaning them. Ruth was currently at the library, and I would take my turn the next two days, so I needed to complete whatever I could. I spent the afternoon walking around the apartment, determining where I would place the new furniture I would purchase whenever I had the funds to do so. Stepping back, I looked at the sight of a cleaned and freshly made bed and thought how strange it would be to spend the night alone in a new place for the first time in my life. Then, I noticed the time and thought I should leave.

Mother had sent a casserole and pie for dinner, and I was bringing it to Ruth and Tobias and baking it in their oven because once Ruth was home from the library, we planned on eating dinner together. I packed up the food and drove to their house. Ruth's car was there already, and because the door was opened, I walked into the kitchen to turn their oven on. I put the pie and the salad I made on the counter and heard loud talking from upstairs. Thinking I would yell to them that I was here and ask if there was anything I could do to help, I began to walk towards the stairs but stopped when I heard the loud conversation.

"Yes, I know that, but Toby, I thought we had agreed about the trips once we were married. Don't you think people will be watching what we do? Things have changed now. You knew they would."

"I didn't say I would *never* be traveling there on weekends; I said I would cut down the quantity of the trips. And what do we care what people think or say? We both have put up with it for years. Let the town gossip. Anyway, it will stop now that we are married."

"We don't know that. We only hope it will. You know we agreed to certain things for this marriage, and I expect you to hold up your end of the bargain."

"Ruth, you know I will. I appreciate the fact that you agreed to marry me. I wanted to keep my job, and this decision is the best for both of us. Why do we need to argue about this again? I said I won't go for a while, and I won't. But I never said I would give it up."

At this point, my foot kicked an unpacked box knocking it over, creating a noise. The talk suddenly stopped, and I thought I better let them know I was here. Eavesdropping again.

I yelled up the stairs, "Hello there! Hi, Ruth and Toby! The door was open, so I came in. I am going to the kitchen to put the casserole in the oven. Mother baked a peach pie too. I'll be there when you get down."

Then I tore into the kitchen and pretended to do what I had already done before Ruth or Tobias entered. I didn't hear anything for

about ten minutes which gave me some time to set the kitchen table
and begin to fill the water glasses. I went over the conversation in my
head. Why didn't Ruth want Toby to travel to see his family? Was she so
possessive? That didn't seem like her. And what agreements were there?
I knew I could not ask anything. I had promised Ruth, so I would need to
ignore what I heard. None of it made sense anyway. At least not then.

We sat together and ate dinner. Ruth gave me a few directives for
things to be done while I took my supervising turn at the library. Because
the schools were closed for a break, there were few students there, and
the library would close early for the rest of the week. That would allow
me to complete whatever organizing in my apartment I had not finished. I
also planned to go out to the farm and help my parents. They had sold the
place and were going to move into town although they didn't yet have a
house. Their move would not take place for a while, but the packing and
sorting had begun.

There was little talk during dinner because both Ruth and Toby
seemed subdued, so I filled the silence explaining both my excitement
and anxiety about being in my first apartment. I explained about the
new furniture I was saving for and my concern about having to cook for
myself. I just continued to talk. After dinner, we ate the peach pie, and I
blabbered on about the new books I had recently ordered. Once there was
nothing more to eat, Ruth thanked me for the dinner and said she and
Toby would clean up the dinner dishes. They sent me on my way, and I
had the feeling that they were anxious for me to go so they could continue their discussion. Quite a honeymoon, I thought, but kept the reflection
to myself and my mouth closed.

***

I didn't see Ruth until the following week, and when I walked
into work on Monday, she was already there and busy. I greeted her, and
the rest of the day, I watched her to determine if I could notice a change
now that she was married. Now that she was *Mrs. Pinkerton*. But she
remained the same person I had known since I was eleven. She also remained *Ruth Evans*. When school children and townspeople came in and
spoke to *Miss Evans*, she did not correct them. None of the placards that
announced her position as head librarian changed. She continued to sign
the orders and checks *Ruth Evans*. Letters and written inquiries which
came to her addressed her as such. As she walked to her home, the one
she shared with her husband, Tobias Pinkerton, I heard the people she
passed and spoke to greet her as *Miss Evans*. She never corrected anyone or changed her name. After a while, I didn't think about her married

name and, while I don't know what the town's gossip mill was discussing, as far as I could tell, everyone just accepted the fact that although she and Tobias were married, she remained Ruth Evans.

Toby and Ruth continued their dinner at Mazie's every Wednesday. They would meet there after work and order the special, and talk, and laugh, and behave as they always had. They attended church most Sundays, sharing the hymnal and harmonizing to *O for a Thousand Tongues to Sing* and *Break Thou the Bread of Life.* They continued their discussions about religions and slavery and morality and ethics and love and honor and greed and good and evil as they applied to literature, and sometimes I was invited to offer my reflections on these subjects and comment on the books we read. They attended the Christmas party given by the combined Everstille Civic Organizations (E.C.O.), and the yearly parades and festivals and events. They did not hold hands or touch in any unsuitable way, but, as a gentleman would, Tobias took Ruth's arm as they crossed the street and helped her up the steps or curb.

No longer did forward young women ask Tobias to accompany them to various concerts or parties or social events, and he no longer needed to be genuinely tender and considerate when turning them down. The marriageable young women in Everstille accepted that they had no chance with him; that there would never be an affirmative answer to their invitations; that just looking at his meaningfully defined jaw and blue Aegean Sea eyes must, in fact, be all they could do, and that needed to be done surreptitiously because Tobias Pinkerton was now taken. He was a married man. Time passed and acceptance about the official marriage of Ruth Evans and Tobias Pinkerton set in.

Life became settled for all of us. I watched as Ruth and Toby established themselves as a married couple, as one of the many young married couples in the town. They moved some furniture around, and ordered a new dining room set from Mitchell's Emporium, and gave a dinner party when it arrived. I attended with Harold in tow and felt utterly grown up wearing my new scarlet dress and matching heels for which I gave up two weeks of groceries. As time passed, I stopped worrying about the marriage of Ruth and Tobias. I forgot the argument I had overheard, and decided that they were as happy as any other married couple I knew.

Tobias and Ruth attended all the Sunday services for months. The winter season was almost over, and spring was on its way when, one Sunday, Ruth and Tobias were not in church. I thought maybe one of them was ill, and I was worried although I had seen Ruth on Friday and she appeared perfectly healthy. I decided to stop at their house and check on them. I drove to their house after the church service and parked in their driveway noting that Toby's car was not there. When Ruth opened the door, I could tell she had been crying, but I didn't mention it.

"I thought you might be ill, Ruth. I didn't see you or Toby at church and was worried. The last time we spoke you said you would see me Sunday in church."

"I'm fine, Anne. Toby went to Chicago for the weekend, and I just didn't feel like going to church. But, thanks for checking on me."

She did not ask me in, and I probed no further. I told her to call if she felt like taking a walk later and drove back to my apartment. When the phone rang in a couple hours, it was Ruth asking me over for tea and a piece of the cinnamon cake she had baked. I returned to her house and was there when it happened.

On Monday, there was a buzz in the town about Tobias and Ruth. Tobias had brought someone back with him from Chicago, and the person was staying at their house. And when Toby or Ruth introduced the man to anyone, they introduced him as Tobias' Chicago cousin, Terrence Douglas.

Terrence Douglas

Like any living and thriving entity, the town of Everstille has certain expectations when it comes to *change*. For example, the Hudson's grandson, Merle, stayed with them every summer for three weeks. The visits continued until Merle was sixteen and refused to come because he would miss his girlfriend and wanted to get a job. However, for nine years, the expectation was that Merle would be around for those three weeks, and the townspeople accepted this.

They expected it, and therefore, prepared for it. Mr. Clampet of Clampet's Groceries would ask Mrs. Hudson if he should order a couple extra jars of that peanut butter Merle liked, and the answer was "Yes, thank you." Sheriff Samms said to Mr. Hudson, "Almost time for that grandson, right?" and Mr. Hudson would answer, "That's right. He's getting bigger every year." The women of the Rachel Circle who ran Vacation Bible School at the church would inquire, "Should we get an extra Bible Coloring Book for Merle this year?" and the grandparents would nod and remark, "Merle just loves your program."

And after it was all over, and Merle had returned home with his parents, evaluation would begin. Mr. Clampet would ask, "Did Merle enjoy those peanut butter sandwiches?" and Mrs. Hudson would nod and answer, "He sure can put them away. Loves my strawberry jam too." And the sheriff would say, "That grandson of yours has sure grown!" and Mr. Hudson would reply, "Almost as tall as me. Next year he will be." Then the Rachel Circle women would comment, "My, your Merle colors well. And he didn't even get into a fight this year." The grandparents would nod and smile at the women and sigh with relief that peace had been maintained. Expectation, preparation, evaluation: the mechanisms of ease and civility.

But that is not what happened when Terrence Douglas came to town. There were no expectations. Not once did either Ruth or Tobias mention that a new member of the family, a Chicago cousin, was coming to stay. No one said to Mazie, "There will be three instead of two for the Wednesday special." Pastor Richards of the Methodist Episcopal Church was not expecting to preach to an extra person during the Sunday services. None of Ruth and Tobias' neighbors expected to see a strange person entering and exiting the old Victorian house. No expectations for anyone in Everstille.

And then, without expectation, how could there be preparation?

Tobias did not go the Clampet's Groceries and purchase three small chicken breasts instead of two. Ruth did not visit Mitchell's Emporium looking for some new towels for the upstairs bathroom or a new set of pillowcases to place on the guest bed. Sheriff Samms was not informed that someone different would be walking down Main Street and driving Tobias' car. No preparation was done. None. And if there was no expectation and no preparation, how could the Everstille community evaluate what was happening? Ease and civility in the town were disturbed.

Instead, that late Sunday afternoon, on the weekend Tobias Pinkerton had made his usual trip to Chicago for a visit with his family, he returned with another person in the passenger seat of his car. Tobias pulled into the driveway, and a strange man got out of the car with him. The two of them began to move boxes and bags and suitcases into the house. Ruth was home, and watched as they brought the belongings into the front hallway, placing them at the bottom of the stairs. I know this because I had come over to have tea and partake of cinnamon cake with her, and she told me that Toby was coming home with his Chicago cousin. We sipped our tea and Ruth served the cake, and we waited for the men to arrive. The neighbors knew this because they were sitting on their various porches enjoying a warm spring Sunday. In a few minutes, additional neighbors had come out on their porches and there it was… without expectation or preparation, the evaluation had begun.

When the moving was completed, Toby brought Terrence into the kitchen and introduced him first to Ruth and then to me. I was surprised that Ruth hadn't met him before, but then, how would she? When Terrence shook her hand, he said, "Thank you, Ruth. I know we will get along, and I am grateful you are allowing me to be here."

I thought his phrase *allowing me to be here*, was an unusual thing to say, but I did not understand the situation at that point. I'm not sure I understand it even now. I was busy studying the Chicago cousin, and as he and Toby sat down at the table for tea and some of the cake Ruth had baked, I was able to look carefully at Terrence Douglas.

I watched him talk casually and easily with Toby as Ruth and I listened, and I thought that surely there could not be two more attractive men around. Tobias, tall and muscular and blond, and Terrence, tall, although not quite the height that Tobias attained, huskier but not heavy, and with hair a hue I had never seen. To label Terrence's hair *red* is to do it injustice. It was the color of a new copper penny but two shades lighter. It shone like the orangey gold of autumn leaves; it was like the last streak on the horizon when there was an auburn/gingery sky at night.

Stripes of gold mixed with flashes of burgundy, and his blue/green/gray eyes struggled to live up to the influence of his locks. I looked at the two men and felt like a small brown mouse, a washed-out, tattered woolen sweater, a collection of burned, used coffee grounds in a cracked cup next to them. I glanced at Ruth and thought she felt the same way as she continued to straighten her dress, brush back the lock of hair continually falling into her face, and scrunch her mouth to the side. Two beauties. Two beasts. I knew which I was.

I did not stay long. I told Terrence I was glad to have met him, and that I would see him around town, and wished them all a good evening as I left for my apartment. I walked out to my car and heard Mrs. Wilson, their neighbor, and the church music director call to me. I turned and yelled *Hello* to her and waved, and pretended I did not see her hand motion to me to come over. I knew what that was about, and I had no intention of standing on Ruth's neighbor's porch gossiping about her. I was sure that Mrs. Wilson would soon be on the telephone spreading the news that some man had appeared to move into the Pinkerton's house. I would not partake in the Sunday afternoon gossip fest that was certain to take place.

The Chicago cousin went to church the next Sunday with Ruth and Toby. I watched (actually, everyone watched) as they came in just before the choir's processional and took their place in their usual pew, three ahead of me. Ruth moved in first, and then Toby, and then Terrence. The congregation stood and sang, and I saw that Ruth held her own hymnal as Toby and his Chicago cousin shared one, and it appeared that their hands, Tobias' right, and Terrence's left, touched underneath the book, but I was three pews back and could have been mistaken. Pastor Richards gave his sermon and led the readings, but I would fail a test about the address if one were given. I was carefully watching three pews ahead and keeping track of how many times the right shoulder of Toby touched the left shoulder of Terrence. Of course, the pews were full, and I may very well have been in error. There were at least two times his left shoulder touched the right shoulder of Ruth. Of that count, I was sure.

Mrs. Wilson sat straight at the organ and introduced the final hymn and led the congregation in singing *Joyful, Joyful, We Adore Thee* as the recessional took place. I listened and heard the lovely harmonizing of two male voices, but Ruth's alto seemed to be much fainter, and there were times I was sure she was not singing, but simply holding her singular hymnal as she looked downward. But then, again, my distance could have fooled me into thinking that, and I tried to pay more attention to my own singing unto the Lord.

People whispered and gossiped and blathered and chattered. All Everstille wondered about the blush-haired Chicago cousin and speculated how long he would be staying with the Pinkertons. Two weeks passed, and when Tobias went after school, to Clampet's Groceries and purchased three chicken breasts, Mr. Clampet just nodded and said, "I hope your guest enjoys these." Then a month went by and Sheriff Samms said to me, "I guess Tobias' Chicago cousin is having a long visit, right?" and I just shrugged and smiled and went on my way. After two months had gone by, and a job opening in the Indiana Phone Company office on Main Street was occupied by the Chicago cousin, Mrs. Wilson spoke to me as she returned a late library book asking, "Well, that Chicago cousin seems to have found a home and a job here in Everstille. What do you think about him living with Ruth and Tobias?" I simply said, "Mrs. Wilson, you owe three cents for the late fee," and ignored her question.

After six months, when Ruth and Tobias and Terrence went together to the Christmas party given by the combined Everstille Civic Organizations (E.C.O.) and both danced with Ruth and with me, the town of Everstille expected it. They were prepared for the trio to enjoy the festivities and sit together. On Wednesday evenings, Mazie set three chairs at the table close to the window, and served three Blue Plate Specials. Dinner parties given by Ruth and Toby featured Terrence as chef, and the invitees evaluated the evenings, giving them the highest marks. It did not take long for Terrence to become established in the town, and while the three of them living together appeared strange to some, most of the townspeople tolerated it, and once again Everstille became tranquil and orderly. As I worked at the library, I heard many remarks about Terrence Douglas, the Chicago cousin, and his capability to move into the life of the town with ease and civility.

Ease and Civility

The town became accustomed to seeing Terrence Douglas walk its streets. He drove Tobias' car to Mackies' Service Station for gas and oil and talked to Mackie, making a friend of him. He happened to walk by the Police Department and saw Sheriff Samms struggling to move a new desk into the office and helped with the task. He visited Clampet's and bought groceries and spoke to Mr. Clampet, and then went to Banter's Drugs and Pharmacy and bought band-aids and hydrogen peroxide because they were needed at home. He was a regular at Peterson's Bakery on Tuesdays when the sour cream donuts were the special, and he never failed to stop in at the library, bringing some delicious treats for Ruth and me. Terrence was poised and polished and polite, and everyone seemed to like him. Except Ruth.

I understood. At least, I thought I did. Ruth and Toby had been married for only a couple years, and they were settling into the old Victorian house, redecorating, and reorganizing, and making it their own. New furniture was ordered and positioned in exactly the right places; the draperies had been updated; a small flower garden was planned at the back of the house in the sunny place which was perfect for the daisies, purple coneflowers, and snapdragons Ruth wanted to plant. And now there was another person to account for. Three pork chops for Friday night dinner. Three seats at the Bijou Theater for the Saturday night film. Three people crammed into an already full church pew. Three. Three is the proverbial crowd. I never questioned Ruth or pried into her personal life with Tobias. I assumed things would work themselves out, although I was not exactly sure what that would mean, and now, here was Terrence.

I am unsure exactly when Ruth changed her mind and attitude. It seemed a long time. Terrence started a job working for the Indiana Telephone Company, and the office was across the street and down a bit from the library. On one Tuesday, in the early morning, he came to the library to drop off the sour cream donuts. I was at the front desk; Ruth was in the back office looking through some invoices, and only one patron was sitting at the far corner table. Terrence came in through the front door, smiled at me, and stopped at the desk.

"Good morning, Anne. Here are some dee-licious treats for you and Ruth. How are you?"

"Good, Terrence, and thank you. Honestly, I think I am putting on weight eating these. They are so good. I love Peterson's donuts."

"I do too. That's a fine bakery. Where is Ruth?"

"She is back in the office doing some paperwork. Don't worry, I won't eat all these! I'll make sure she gets at least one."

Terrence smiled and did not make a move to leave. "I think I'll go and say good morning to her."

I thought this strange. After all, didn't they live in the same house? Hadn't they just seen each other a short while ago? Didn't they eat their oatmeal at the same table? Terrence stood for a second, stroking the desk gently with his hand and chewing his side lip. I watched as he wandered through the stacks which led to the back room. On other Tuesdays, when he dropped off the donuts to me at the front desk, he would then leave to go to work. This was new.

I listened as Terrence knocked on the office door and then went in. Not that I was eavesdropping, and anyway, with the door closed, I couldn't learn much. I strained to hear but only quiet murmurs seeped through the wooden door, and then, suddenly, Ruth laughed. Terrence did too. After another minute or so, he came back to the front, said good-bye, and left. I was curious, but could not ask anything. However, in an hour or so, when Ruth came out of the office with some letters to be mailed, she was smiling.

That was the day I noticed the bond between Terrence and Ruth had changed. I don't know why, or what, or how, but I saw that their relationship, which I thought of as cool at best, had warmed up. I thought this was most likely a good thing; that for as long as he was going to stay with Toby and Ruth, they would need to get along. At that time, I was under the impression that eventually Terrence would find a place to stay, then move out and allow the Pinkertons to have their own lives. I was mistaken.

A couple of Sundays later, as I waited in my usual pew at church and listened to the Bach Prelude performed by Mrs. Wilson, Toby and Ruth and Terrence walked into their pew. In that order. Ruth was between the two men, taking a position I hadn't seen before. The three of them sat as a familiar group, and Ruth's left shoulder touched Toby's right shoulder while her right met Terrence's left. As they stood to sing *For the Beauty of the Earth*, Ruth held the hymnal out, and the three of them glanced at the well-known words and sang out in a harmonizing trio of voices. Something had changed.

I started to notice the three of them together. A few weeks

later, it was my turn to work the Saturday shift at the library. I closed at the usual noon hour and crossed the street to get to Clampet's where I would pick up needed groceries. I looked at the trio walking ahead and across the street from me and saw that Ruth was walking between Toby and Terrence and had her arms linked through theirs. They were entering Mitchell's Emporium, and as they reached the store's large door, Terrence opened it and smiled at Ruth as she went in, and as Tobias entered, he reached out and squeezed Terrence's arm. They smiled at each other, and then Terrence followed them into the store. I thought that it was a splendid thing that the three of them were getting along. That the three of them seemed to be happy. That the three of them appeared an established alliance. That the three of them…and then I began to wonder about the three of them. I was naïve, and still to some extent am, but I speculated, and conjectured, and deliberated about things I probably should not have. And then I thought that if I were doing this, who else is doing the same?

I began to watch Ruth and listen more carefully to her. Perhaps I could discern what was happening, what had changed, what was going on in the large Victorian house that she and her husband and his Chicago cousin inhabited. But I could not determine any differences except that she and Terrence were getting along, and apparently the three of them were content with whatever their living situation had become. I decided that I was turning into one of the town's old gossiping biddies and determined to stop hypothesizing and worry about my own life and job.

During this time, Tobias had gained a measure of fame in the education community. After the war, when Everstille's veterans had returned home, he had proposed a strategy which allowed those who had quit school, to receive their high school diplomas. While the plan was only semi-successful, Tobias eventually wrote an article about it and to his surprise, it was accepted for publication in *The Journal of Experimental Education*. The ideas in the article gained a bit of notoriety and initiated speaking engagements for him. He received invitations to speak at various school board meetings and principal seminars which meant Toby began to do some traveling.

His traveling left Ruth and Terrence by themselves. I noticed that during the weekends Toby was gone, the two of them would walk, arm in arm, to the Bijou for the Saturday night film. They went shopping together at Clampet's, each of them going home carrying a bag of groceries. They used Ruth's car and traveled out Smokehouse Road to Elkhart because Ruth needed to purchase new shoes at a special store there. And on Sunday, they sat together in the pew a bit ahead of me, where I watched as they shared the hymnal and sang, *He Leadeth Me, Oh Blessed Thought,* in a lovely harmonizing duet. I thought that Ruth's left-hand touched Terrence's right hand beneath the hymnal, but then I was three pews away and could have been mistaken.

Life continued. Time passed, and expectations, preparations, and evaluations about Ruth, Tobias, and the Chicago cousin were finalized. Everstille accepted that the three of them lived together and apparently, they were content. I accepted it too.

Besides, new and exciting changes were taking place. The City Council, Library Board, and town's leading citizens had decided that a new and larger library building was necessary. After months and months of planning and budgeting, the work to expand the current building and build additional rooms was underway. Ruth and I were functioning around the noise and clutter of the workmen, and of necessity, library hours and days had been shortened until the project was completed. To avoid screeching at each other over the chaos of moving and hammering and sawing, we had decided to start work at an earlier hour, before the workmen arrived, so that we could plan and organize our days with less disorder.

One morning, before the library opened, we were talking about the plans, and I was expressing my opinion about the new Research Room that was, I thought, an excellent idea. I was speaking fervently about it, not paying attention to Ruth's unhealthy complexion and was unprepared when she ran away from me and into the bathroom when she rid herself of her morning coffee and oatmeal.

I followed and said. "Ruth, what's wrong? Are you ill? Should I call the doctor?"

I watched as she washed her hands and patted some water on her face. She stared at her reflection in the mirror, and turned and studied me. I couldn't determine what her expression meant. She took a deep breath and let it out slowly in an audible sigh. Then she looked at me with un-fathomable green cat eyes and said,

"No, Anne. I'm pregnant."

Pregnant

I stood still as thoughts pulsed through my head at breakneck speed. Toby and Ruth must have worked through whatever problems they had. They must be truly husband and wife. I was pretty sure I knew what this meant; after all, I had grown up on a farm. There were additional questions. When was the baby due? What would this mean for Ruth's library job? Would I still have a job? What should I say to her? And then I said,

"Congratulations, Ruth! I'm so happy for you. This is exciting news. I am sure Toby is thrilled. Are you feeling O.K.? I mean, I know sometimes the mornings are bad. Have you seen Doctor Grenville yet?" The questions tumbled out of me, and I expected answers to tumble out of Ruth.

Ruth's answer was quietly given and surprising. "Anne, I need you to keep this between us. You know because you caught me being sick. No, Toby does not know yet. No, I haven't seen the doctor; you are the only one who knows right now."

I was dumbfounded, and I stood there with a gaping mouth. Ruth's green eyes appeared sad, and I wondered if she would explain herself. I was not sure what comment to make, so I said nothing. She sighed once again and then motioned me into her office. She pulled out a chair for me; then she shut the door and took the seat behind her desk even though it was early in the morning, and we were the only people there.

"Anne, this pregnancy is new. I believe I am only a few weeks along and want to wait to talk to Toby. I will see Doctor Grenville in a while, but I need you to not tell anyone at all. You know that I love this job. Once the Library Board finds out I am pregnant, I'll be expected to turn in my resignation. I want to continue working because the new library is important to me, and I want to see it through. I think I will be able to work through the holidays and into the new year, and if I can avoid telling the Library Board until then, I will. I believe I'm due sometime next May. I trust you and need your help keeping this quiet. I can depend on you, can't I?"

"Ruth, you know you can. I'll be quiet. I am just worried about you. Are you well?"

"I'm fine. I've been reading and doing research, and this

morning sickness should not last more than another few weeks. I know I can depend on you, Anne, but in a couple of months I might need you to cover for me at events at the high school or some meetings. I'm going to try to stay out of the limelight for a while. Eventually the town will know about this, but until then, this is our secret. I'm hoping you will you agree to that. Will you?"

Of course I would, and I told her so. I was pleased that Ruth trusted me with this secret, and I pledged my silence to her and then, not sure what to ask and whether I should even ask anything, went back to the Circulation Desk, and finished the filing I had started. I had no idea how I could help Ruth. I would soon find out.

I continued coming into the library early, but Ruth always seemed to be there before me. We talked about the daily tasks and planned and organized what we could before the workers started their pounding and hammering, and moving furniture and books. I continued to work in the front while Ruth kept to her small office. Because we had shortened days and hours, there were only a few patrons during the morning, and it was after school hours that there were more people, usu-ally school children, around. That left me with quite a bit of time while I filed and worked at tasks that did not require much thinking, to reflect upon the situation with Ruth and Toby. And Terrence.

A year ago, Mrs. Ethel Pinkerton, Toby's mother, died. He and Ruth took some days to travel to Chicago for the funeral, but Terrence did not go. I wondered at the time why he stayed here. After all, if Toby and he were cousins, wasn't Mrs. Pinkerton his aunt? Or maybe not. But wouldn't he go anyway just to pay his respects? When Ruth returned from Chicago, I asked her about this. She appeared perturbed at my question. Which, upon reflection, was none of my business. Then she said something about Terrence being related through the other side, Mr. Pinkerton's family, and that there were bad feelings between the families because of some old argument, and didn't I have those overdue fines to settle and organize? I got the hint and walked to the desk and picked up the fine list.

That drudged up an additional memory. Toby used to travel every month or so to Chicago to see his family. His mother's funeral was the first trip he had taken in a long while. Except for the educational semi-nars he sometimes traveled to on weekends, I could not remember him taking any Chicago trips since that long-ago weekend when he returned from a trip with Terrence. I thought back over the past. No, Toby had not gone to Chicago to visit his sisters and their families. Ruth always told me about those visits. He had been in Everstille every weekend for a long time. Since the funeral. The funeral that Terrence, his Chicago cousin, did not attend. I had this new insight into the relationship between Ruth and Toby and Terrence. I was not exactly sure what it meant, but there was something there. And I could not, would not, ask Ruth. She trusted me with her greatest secret. One of them anyway.

I kept my contemplations to myself. There was no one I would or could talk to about this. I had a few friends, but no one particularly close. Besides, most of the women in Everstille who were my age, married soon after high school and started their own families. As a single woman (spinster? old-maid?), I was discounted except for the times I ran into my old friends at Clampet's where their children were running around, and they were complaining about the price of hamburger meat and milk. Harold, my sometimes beau, had finally given up on me and married one of our high school friends, and I was happy for them. My life was mostly the library and books. I visited my parents, and my sister and brothers and their families. I went to church most Sundays, and attended most civic events and festivities because I was expected to. Anyway, I couldn't wonder out loud about these things. I would be no better than the town gossips.

And then there was the absence of *Donut Tuesday*. Terrence stopped coming into the library to deliver donuts a few weeks ago. One Tuesday I was late getting to work and had skipped breakfast. *There will be donuts soon*, I thought, but the morning passed, and Ruth remained in her office and Terrence hadn't shown up, and my stomach was growling. About eleven that morning, the library was empty, and I walked over to Ruth's office.

"Ruth, Terrence hasn't been in on Tuesdays with donuts for a couple of weeks now. Is everything alright?"

Ruth looked up and I noticed that she had dark circles under her eyes which looked red-rimmed, and it appeared as though she had been crying. She stared at me for a few seconds, and I worried that I had, again, stumbled into something that was not my business. She pushed back in her chair and exhaled

"Everything is fine, Anne. Terrence is just not bringing in the do-nuts because he needs to get to work, and we don't really need all those sweets. Sorry you miss them. I just didn't think about saying anything to you."

"That's fine, Ruth, but I missed breakfast, and I'm hungry. It's quiet here now, and I'm going to run over to Mazie's for a quick sandwich. Do you want something for lunch? I'll pick it up for you."

"If Mazie has that chicken soup ready, I'll take a cup of that. Thanks. I'll sit at the front desk until you return."

I left for Mazie's but first visited Peterson's Bakery where I picked up a few donuts. I did miss them. When I returned, I brought Ruth her soup in a bag and placed a couple of the sweets that neither of us really needed in it. When she took it to her office in the back, I heard her laugh as she opened the bag. It was good to hear Ruth's laugh. There hadn't been much laughing or even smiling lately. I thought she would be happy and thrilled with the coming baby. I assumed we would talk about the plans she and Toby had for their child, perhaps reviewing baby names, and looking together at Dr. Spock's *Baby and Child Care,* but she just seemed stressed and agitated. I was worried about her.

***

The early fall was a demanding one. Toby was occupied with the start of the school session and the plans for the annual Fall Festival and homecoming activities. He was busy with committee meetings and after-school gatherings, and every now and then, he still spoke at seminars. Ruth and I worked at the library and found that shortening the days and hours did not give us more free time. There were boxes of books that needed to be catalogued and prepared for the stacks, and because most of the library furniture was pushed closely together, there was little room to accommodate new holdings. There was also an almost daily delivery of new furniture which needed to be stored somewhere. We were continually pushing things around, trying to make some room. Magazines and periodicals were piling up all over. Then there was the process of hiring additional personnel to work part-time once the new library was complete. The place was in general disarray.

And Terrence? I rarely saw him. The third church pew in front of me was often empty. Ruth and Terrence filled it during the early fall when Toby was absent, busy fulfilled his speaking engagements. A few times, Ruth and Toby appeared together, taking their seats. But the threesome had not made a joint appearance for months. Ruth had made it clear to me that she would gradually fall out of sight so as not to encourage gossip and alert the Library Board once her condition was noticeable. When the week of the Fall Festival and homecoming loomed, she called me into her office and asked me to substitute for her at some of the events.

"Anne, I am hoping you will go to the homecoming dance and be both my substitute and a chaperone. I am not showing yet, but I need to start fading out of sight. If anyone asks, the excuse I told Toby to give was that there were so many tasks to accomplish for the library that I needed to work at it so the completion of the building and reorganization would not be held up. I know this is a weak excuse, but it's the best I can come up with. And I am hoping that should you be questioned as to why *you* cannot complete the work, you will say that there were reports and papers that only the Head Librarian could complete. Will this be O.K.?"

"Yes, of course, I'll be happy to help out and to say whatever you think is best. Will you be at any of the celebrations?"

"Actually, I think I will be able to show up for a while at the parade. It will be noisy and busy, and I can wave to those who will be looking for me before I disappear and go home. Thanks, Anne, I knew I could count on you."

"Happy to help," and then I asked a question which I knew beforehand was none of my business.

"How is Toby? Is he over the moon about the baby? I have not said anything to him, but then I haven't seen him in a while. I know he has been busy with work. What does Terrence think about this? I was trying to figure out exactly what his relationship will be to the baby. Second cousin? Maybe third cousin? I am unsure how that works."

There was a silence on Ruth's part that let me know I had tread on ground that was not mine to walk on. However, I really did wonder about the questions. I knew Ruth was close to forty, and would be forty by the time the baby was born, and Toby was a few years younger than Ruth. They would be older parents, and I wondered how this would affect their lives. And Terrence's. I also wondered if Terrence was going to continue living with them, but I thought that if there was a question that was truly none of my business, that was it. Ruth looked pained as she answered.

"Toby is happy, of course, and so is Terrence. And speaking of Terrence, would you mind if the two of you go to the dance together? Toby wants Terrence there to help chaperone, and as long as you are going also…"

I was surprised at this suggestion, but thought it was a reasonable one, so I agreed. I did not know until later that lately, Terrence's lack of female companionship was being noticed and remarked on by others. His bachelorhood was under discussion at various committee meetings including the Rachel Circle and Everstille Women's Organization, and the talk was getting back to Toby and Ruth. This was Ruth's effort to keep gossip at bay. She positioned Terrence and I together so that the town would infer we were a newfound couple who spontaneously and voluntarily found each other's company and reveled in it. So, Terrence and I went to the homecoming dance together as chaperones, and I began, albeit at first innocently and unsuspectingly, to join Ruth and Toby and Terrence in what I later began to think of as a friendly conspiracy.

Friendly Conspiracy

Do not misunderstand. I thoroughly enjoy the company of Terrence Douglas. He is considerate, intelligent, and amusing, and had he interest in any kind of a romantic relationship, I might have considered it too. However, neither one of us had such inclinations, although for different reasons. But we enjoyed each other's company, and it was comfortable being with Ruth and Toby, and for a while, their threesome turned into our foursome.

After the homecoming dance, Terrence walked me home, and we spoke of important private issues. Some, I knew; some, I suspected; some, shocked me. I asked if Toby and Ruth knew he was telling me their secrets, and he said they did; they had discussed it, and Ruth assured them I was trustworthy and would keep the information to myself. And I did. However, the biggest secret, the one that none of them could admit to, remained hidden. I was not told it then, but in time, during the following spring, when life changed for all of us, I discovered it. In the end, it was fairly obvious.

By its nature, a conspiracy requires planning, and Terrance and I planned our outings. At first, I felt as if I were an actress, as if I were playing a part in the high school drama club performance. But it didn't take long for me to become nervous about what we were doing. I realized that we were all, especially me because I was an obliging player, participating in the flaunting of traditional, accepted conventions and norms. We were engaged in, at the least, duplicity and deceit, and at the most, prohibited, illicit, and (in certain states) criminal actions. But my concern, and love, and friendship for Ruth, my mentor and friend, won out. I had agreed to play along and remain silent about their reality, and I would honor my word.

The homecoming dance was on September 26, the last Saturday in September. We created a calendar to be seen in public during the following four months. Once the winter and cold and snow came, Ruth could hide her condition in sweaters and shawls as we all did for warmth. When I remember back to the events, there were fewer than I thought. As I remember, these were the occasions Terrence and I took part in as a couple:

One Friday night fish fry at Mazie's

Two Saturday afternoon shopping trips up and down Main Street

Three times we knew we would be seen together. And, frankly, I had a delightful time at them, and I believe Terrence did too. There were no displays of affection between us, no hand holding, no deep looks and longing eyes. We agreed that if we behaved just as what we were… friends…that would be enough, and apparently it was. Terrence, just as any gentleman would, took my elbow as I stepped up on the curb, held my arm as we crossed with traffic, held the door for me as I went into a building. Frankly, it was not much different than the times Ruth and I spent doing the same things.

Then there were a few times the four of us were seen out together. They included:

One dinner party at the Pinkerton house given for faculty

One early fall evening when we were seen getting into a car and traveling down Smokehouse Road to Elkhart for a concert

One Sunday evening pot-luck dinner at the Methodist Episcopal Church

Six times was more than enough for the town to believe that finally, Terrence Douglas had found someone and would eventually settle down to live a normal, traditional, accepted life. The two of us would eventually marry and probably have a child or two and find a place to live in Everstille where we would raise our child/children and take part in the events of a normal, traditional, accepted family. And it was about time too. That *ménage à trois* that was going on in the Pinkerton house, Chicago cousin or not, was just this side of being indecent. Brows were wiped, disappointed sighs from the town's marriageable young women were heard, and expectation, planning and evaluation were considered complete.

Even my mother was fooled. My parents sold their farm and property on Smokehouse Road to the Goodwin Construction and Building Company and moved to town. They bought Mrs. Beckett's dilapidated Victorian house two streets away from Clampet's Groceries partly because it *was* dilapidated, and would give Dad some work to complete and keep him busy since he no longer had the farm. The house had been emptied for almost two years, since Mrs. Beckett's death, and no one wanted it. There were even discussions about tearing it down, but Mother and Dad examined the place, said it had "good bones", bought it, and began the process of rehabilitation. Mother was particularly pleased with the small room she called the *library* because it had built-in book cases on two of the walls, and she was excited about obtaining additional books and making the room hers. I usually saw my parents once a week, scrutinized Dad's recent carpentry project, and Mother's reorganization of her library, and stayed for supper. Two weeks before Thanksgiving, she and I were washing the supper dishes and talking.

"Anne Olivia," and when she used my middle name, I knew she was going to say something she thought crucial, "when were you going to tell us about your current young suitor? I have heard from two neighbors and Mrs. Wilson from church about your outings with him."

Well, the plan is at least working and people are noticing. I thought. Also, her adjective, *current*, was a kindness on her part since there had been few suitors over the past ten years.

"Mother, if you are talking about Terrence Douglas, we are simply friends. I've known him since he moved here from Chicago to live with Ruth and Toby. We just found it convenient to do some things together. I usually go with Ruth, but she has been so busy with the new library that we just haven't had time to get together outside of work." *And now I have also worked in an excuse for Ruth's absence.*

"Why don't you invite Terrence for Thanksgiving dinner? We will all be here, and it will be a wonderful time. He can meet all the family, and we can get to know him. There is always plenty of food, and Dad and I would like to talk to him."

Great. I sighed inwardly. I knew this could be a problem, *Mother has me married off now.*

"Thanks for the offer, Mother, but I am fairly sure Terrence and Ruth and Toby have plans of their own. However, I will pass your invitation along. Just don't expect me to bring Terrence or anyone else to the family get-together. He and I are friends, and that is all."

"The offer stands. Make sure you ask him. He does seem a nice young person, and such lovely red hair!"

We finished the dishes and Mother pressed a couple of sandwiches and some cookies into my arms as I left. I kissed her cheek, went to find Dad to say good-night, and left for my own apartment.

***

Two weeks later Thanksgiving came. I showed up at my parents holding my most recent accomplishment: a mandarin orange-mini-marshmallow Jell-O mold. When I came into their house, I could see the disappointment on Mother's face. I assumed it was because I was alone and not because of the mandarin orange-mini-marshmallow Jell-O mold, which except for the cookies I could bake, was my only real culinary achievement. One I was able to repeat two weeks later at the Methodist Episcopal Church's annual Christmas pot-luck.

Christmas Pot-Luck

Many years ago, someone at church came up with the idea to combine the church choir's Christmas musical program with a Christmas party and a pot-luck dinner, and it continues to be a popular yearly event. I remember going with my parents and siblings; then Ruth and I attended together, and then Ruth and Toby showed up. The last couple years it was Ruth and Toby and Terrence, and this year, I joined them. Ruth (vegetable casserole) and I (mandarin orange mini-marshmallow Jell-O mold) came in with Toby and Terrence (olive loaf from Clampet's with Peterson Bakery's white bread loafs for sandwiches) and greeted everyone as they entered. My mother and father (chiffon cake and baking powder biscuits) were just finishing setting up the long tables where everyone was placing their dishes.

"Cold dishes here, hot dishes at this end, and the desserts will go on that table over there," Mrs. Wilson (tuna noodle casserole topped with potato chips), Ruth's neighbor and the church music director, was anxiously directing the traffic into the church basement, using the same strident voice with which she directed the choirs.

"If your dessert needs to be refrigerated until later, please take it to the kitchen and Mrs. Richards will find a place for it," and the forceful voice continued the directives.

Mrs. Richards (another tuna noodle casserole but this one was topped with bread crumbs) was Pastor Richards' subdued and modest wife who had been relegated to kitchen duty by Mrs. Wilson, who placed her own casserole first in the line of hot foods. Mrs. Richards' casserole was behind the two green bean casseroles (Mrs. Beacon and Mrs. Anderson) and next to the spicy baked three-bean dish (Mrs. Jackson). Right after Mrs. Wilson's tuna casserole, was the large, pineapple-covered, thinly-sliced baked ham that the Clampet's delivered and, as the attendees came in, was eyed by all. The cauldron of Sloppy Joes and the tower of buns (Mr. and Mrs. Chessworth) and the Spam sandwiches (Mr. and Mrs. Banter) would be eaten by the children who had their own table filled with goodies including potato chips (Ian MacKenzie of Mackie's Gas Station and Garage) and various home-baked cookies (Mrs. Samms, Mrs. Johnson. Miss Gwen Hoffsteader), and would certainly keep them quiet and munching away for a while.

Once everyone was in and coats and hats were hung up on the large rack just outside the basement's reception area, Pastor Richards gave a short welcome. Then he gave a much longer blessing than most people thought was necessary, and finally, the food line was free to start. Everyone filled plates and found seats at the long tables that the husbands of the Rachel Circle had set up earlier in the afternoon. As Ruth and Toby and Terrence and I found seats for ourselves, I saw my parents walking over to take the two seats close to us. I was worried. I did not want my mother to begin a conversation and ask Terrence what his intentions were and when she could start looking forward to seeing her red-haired grandchildren. I tried giving my mother a look, but she totally ignored me, and as they sat down, my father started to eat heartily and comment on each dish as he took a bite. I was grateful for his running commentary but knew it would not last. My mother sat down after greeting everyone around her and took a few polite bites before beginning the very conversation I feared she would.

"Well, isn't it wonderful to see you four young people together having such a good time. Mr. Douglas, I am not sure we have formally met. I am Anne's mother, and this is her father," and she nodded to my dad who looked up, chewing, and waving with the hand that was holding a baking powder biscuit. My mother, however, leaned across the table and held her hand out to Terrence who took it and smiled at her.

"I can see where Anne's lovely eyes come from," said Terrence, and with this comment, my mother beamed. She glanced at me and the look in her eyes said *I knew I would get to meet your new beau somehow*! I quietly sighed and took a few bites of the honey baked apple (Sarah Jones) on my plate.

"Anne said you had other plans for Thanksgiving dinner, but I want you to know you're welcome to come for Christmas." I looked quickly at Terrence and glanced sideways at Ruth and Toby who were doing their best to ignore the conversation and concentrated on consuming the potato salad (Janet Lynn Everett) and chicken croquettes (Mrs. Tremble) on their plates.

"Thank you, Mrs. Rivens, but I do have plans for Christmas. You are kind to ask, however," and Terrence cut into his piece of ham (the Clampets) and speared a bite of yams baked with marshmallows (Mrs. Jason Wicks) and chewed.

"Just in case things change, you are always welcome. Ruth, how is the library expansion going?"

I was grateful for the change of topic and rolled my eyes at Terrence who grinned and raised his eyebrows. We continued eating and listened to Ruth and my mother discuss the library changes and plans. When the dessert table and large coffee pots were brought out, I excused myself to get a piece of the pineapple upside-down cake (Mazie of Mazie's Restaurant) that I really didn't want, but used as an excuse to leave the table. My mother followed me.

"Anne, you didn't ask Terrence if he wanted dessert. You could bring some back to him."

"Mother, he is perfectly capable of getting his own. Besides, he's still eating dinner."

"It would be the considerate thing to do. And I am so happy to see you out together. He has the loveliest hair and seems such a gentleman."

I looked at my mother and said, "Please, just stop!" I took my pineapple cake dessert back and plopped it down in front of Terrence. I couldn't eat it.

Terrence gave me a questioning look, shrugged his shoulders, and began to eat the cake. This day couldn't be over soon enough, but there was the clean-up and the Senior and Junior Choir Christmas Concert to get through. Everyone completed their dessert and coffee while the choir members, led by Mrs. Wilson, left to prepare for their performance. Once the church basement was straightened, leftover food wrapped, and tables and chairs placed back into the long storage closet, everyone went up to the sanctuary to hear the concert which, to be fair to Mrs. Wilson, was lovely. The concert completed, Pastor Richards gave, thankfully, a short speech and blessing, and we left for our homes. Ruth and I covered our heads with our scarves, and I held her arm so she would not fall during what was an escalating snowstorm.

My car was parked at Ruth's house, and we all crowded into hers and drove there. I said good-night to the three of them, got into my car and drove carefully back to my apartment while the snow turned to sleet and ice. I opened the door and had just placed the remains of my Jell-O mold into the ice- box when the telephone rang. It was my mother.

"Hello Anne, I just wanted to check and make sure you were home and safe. This snowstorm is going to be something."

"Mother, I am fine. Are you and Dad O.K.?"

"We are good. Anne, I really think Terrence is a nice young man and I am so happy for you both. Will you see him at Christmas? You know, I certainly meant what I said about having him here then. Why don't you talk to him and ask him again?"

I took a deep breath and told myself to be calm. "Mother, we are just friends. I know he had plans for the holidays and no, I will not ask him again for Christmas. Now, please, stop with the match-making."

We spoke for a minute or two about the evening's events and then hung up. I knew my mother wanted me to be married like my sister, and I hated to disappoint her, but there was no doubt that it would never be to Terrence Douglas. I was not sure there would be a marriage to any-one. I looked out the window and watched the icy snow fall. It would be a white Christmas this year.

I readied for sleep and placed an extra blanket on the bed where I lay awake for a long time thinking about the evening, my parents, the coming holiday season, and the secrets I was keeping for Ruth and Toby and Terrence. As I lay in bed listening to the wind, cuddled under the blankets piled on top of me, I thought back to the last few months. Soon there would be a new year; one, which I did not know then, would bring a change in my life and the lives of those around me. I fell asleep won-dering about the future, about the coming new year of 1954.

1954

The icy snow fell and melted and fell and melted again. The middle of December brought the biggest snowstorm of the year, and then it shifted to a typical Indiana winter. I lived close enough to the library so some days when the snow was piled high on my car, and the streets were dangerously slippery, I walked there, bundled in multiple scarves and the warmest sweaters I could find. Because of Ruth's pregnancy, I offered to open and close the library and encouraged her to come in later. There weren't many patrons during the cold winter, and the shortened days usually brought reduced hours of operation anyway. Ruth took advantage of my offer and told me she was grateful.

Christmas was a wonderful time with my family. We gathered on Christmas Day at Josh's newly built house, and there was, as usual, too much food, too much talk, and too much noise from all the grandchildren. Only once did mother ask about Terrence, and I looked at her and said "Stop, Mother", and, surprisingly, she did.

The week between Christmas and New Year's Day was arctic, and the remaining snow kept people at home. On Thursday, the day before New Year's Eve, Ruth called early in the morning to tell me she would not be in and to consider closing early.

"Are you feeling O.K?" I asked.

"I am fine, Anne. I just feel lazy and am tired. Besides how many people were there yesterday? Or the day before? You know this is the slow time of year. Whatever paperwork I must complete can wait a few days. Why don't you close at three?"

"I probably will, as long as there is no one here."

"What are you doing tomorrow night? Are you going to be with your family? I know you often get together on New Year's Eve."

"Not this year. Josh's little one is sick with a cold, and Mother thinks Dad might have caught it, and everyone just wants to cuddle with their own families, so we are staying separate. We thought we might get together for a family dinner later in January. I have no plans for the night."

"Good. Then plan on coming here. Toby and Terrence and I are going to stay in and play card games. Come on over in the afternoon and we'll cook dinner together. I'm taking over the cooking from Terrence, and I have a new recipe and could use your help. Pack an overnight bag and stay here. We'll see the New Year in together, and Terrence said he'll make his special buttermilk pancakes for all of us in the morning. Besides, I also have something to show you."

"Thanks, Ruth. That sounds like a good time. I can make some cookies tomorrow morning and bring them. Will that be fine?"

"Sounds wonderful, Anne. Also, before you leave, look through the new books and pick one that you think I would like. I need something to read. Just make sure they are good stories…you know what I think. Thanks, and I'll see you about four tomorrow afternoon."

We hung up, and I went to the *New Book Section* and took *Fahrenheit 451* and J.D. Salinger's *Nine Stories* and placed the books into my bag which was behind the Circulation Desk. Then I printed out two large signs which advertised the early closing and a reminder about the closure through the weekend, and taped them to the front door and the side window. There was no need to worry about chasing any patrons out, because the last one left just after noon. I bundled up, locked up, and stopped at Clampet's on my way home for a few needed items to bake the cookies in the morning.

The following day, New Year's Eve morning, I got up early and baked both chocolate chip and oatmeal raisin cookies which I wrapped to take to Ruth's house. A bit before four in the afternoon, I drove carefully to the house, parked on the recently shoveled driveway, and carried in my cookies, Ruth's books, and my packed overnight bag. Ruth opened the door and took the cookies from me while I took off my boots and coat and hat and placed everything in the front closet. I handed Ruth the books I brought for her and she smiled as she looked at them. We went into the kitchen where the ingredients for a *Hoppin' John* dish were ready to assemble.

"According to something I read, it's supposed to be good luck for the new year to eat this dish. I found a simple recipe and made it for dinner tonight. We could all use some good luck," Ruth explained to me. "Do you mind cutting the celery and pepper? I already have the onions chopped, but need to fry up this bacon. The rice is almost done."

We worked at our tasks and got the dish together. Ruth mixed up the cornbread she would serve with the casserole, and then made tea for us. We sat down at the kitchen table, and she pulled over the cookies.

"I know I don't need any, but one would be good with this tea."

"Where are Toby and Terrence?"

"Toby went to the school to complete his daily check on the building, and Terrence drove to Mazie's for a bottle of wine. I won't imbibe, but he thought a glass to welcome in the new year would be nice tonight. Would you like one of your cookies with the tea?"

"Maybe one of the chocolate chips. My favorite! Wine. I think I have only had it twice before. Sounds like a great thing to help bring in the new year."

"Anne, finish your cookie, and then let me show you what we have been doing over the past weeks."

I took the last bite and washed it down with some tea and looked at Ruth. "What is it?"

She pushed back her chair. As she did so, I could tell that on Ruth's slender frame there was a small rounded area in the front. Until I saw that, the baby was an abstract idea. Suddenly, it was reality. She motioned to the back of the kitchen where there were two doors. The first one we moved past was a large walk-in pantry. Then she opened the other door.

She switched on the light, and we walked into a large room which was in the last stages of being cleaned and painted. A bed, a night-stand, a small table and chairs, and a desk were pushed to one side.

"What is this?"

"Originally this was a room for the housekeeper and has been unused for years. But I talked Toby and Terrence into cleaning and paint-ing it, and when it's done, I am planning on using it as a *birthing room.*"

I looked at Ruth, and she laughed.

"I am planning on a home birth, and this is where the baby will be born."

"Ruth, is that wise? Many women are now going to the hospi-tal for baby births. Isn't that what you should do? Josh's wife had little Amy in the hospital, stayed about a week, and they are both fine. Are you sure you should? What does Doctor Grenville say? You talked with him, didn't you?"

Ruth walked over to the window facing the side of the house and looked out at the snow piled around the house. Then she turned.

"No, I haven't informed the doctor of my plans yet, but I have been doing some research about hospital births, and I think this will be fine. Only about half the women in this town have gone to the hospital, and this is what I decided will be best for the baby and me. Toby and Terrence are helping with the redecorating, and everything will be ready in plenty of time. I just wanted you to see it. What do you think?"

"I didn't know this room was here. It certainly is much larger than a hospital room, and I don't really know much about this stuff. I guess if the doctor thinks it's fine, it is. I like the soft green walls."

We spoke about where the furniture would go and the fact that the room is close to the kitchen and not far from the downstairs bathroom. We left the room, and as Ruth closed the door, we heard someone come in.

"Hello. Where are you?" Terrence called out and then entered the kitchen with a bag he placed on the table. "Smells like good cooking in here. I'm hungry too. Cookies! Great!" and he grabbed one of them in each hand and bit into the first one. He chewed quickly and took more bites and smiled.

I glanced at Ruth. She had a large smile on her face and her green eyes were shining. *Well*, I thought, *I guess they are truly friends now*. Terrence came over to her and gave her a hug and held his one cookie-less hand out to shake mine.

"Glad you're here, Anne. Looking forward to seeing the new year in with us? I am just going to get out the cards and the Monopoly game, but is there anything you need me to do before that?"

"No, thanks, Terrence. We are just going to check the dinner and set the table. I was showing Anna the birthing room and the painting that is being done."

Terrence nodded and left. I wanted to ask Ruth about him and their new, close friendship, but decided to be quiet. After all, I had promised not to ask questions. We continued with dinner, set the table, and Ruth took the bottle out of the bag.

"I don't know much about wine, but I think red is served at room temperature, so I will just leave this here. I wish we had some wine glasses, but the juice glasses will have to do. Would you get three of them out of the cabinet there and wash them up? Thanks, Anne."

As we worked Ruth continued to talk about the library and

the renovations. Because of the weather and the holiday, the outside work had stopped and when the workmen came back in the beginning of January, they would begin additional work inside. It was going to be even noisier, and we would become more crowded. There would be additional changes in the hours and the services provided, and we talked about what would happen in the coming months when Ruth knew she would be expected to resign because of her pregnancy.

The evening was pleasant and enjoyable. We all relished the lucky casserole and cornbread, and Ruth and I cleaned up the dishes while Toby and Terrence set up the table in the dining room for the card games and Monopoly. The plate of cookies was set on the table, and we laughed and played until almost midnight and then put the cards and game away. Terrence went into the kitchen to open the wine and pour three glasses. He brought them into the dining room for us along with some apple cider for Ruth. Midnight came and we toasted each other and wished for a happy and healthy new year.

"I am tired, and I am guessing you are too, Anne," and Ruth smiled at me. "There is a bedroom upstairs or the sofa in the front parlor is comfortable and it's in front of the fireplace which will be warm. Where would you like to be?"

"The fireplace sounds great. I can set up there. I used to sleep in front of ours on the old farm during the cold nights and would like to relive that warmth."

Everyone got up and Toby said to Ruth, "I'll clean things up and you can get Anne settled. Terrence, would you check the fireplace in the parlor? I think it's fine, but could use some more wood."

We left to complete our tasks. I went to the front closet to remove my bag and set up in the parlor where Terrence had made sure there was a warm fire. He wished us a good-night and walked up the stairs to his room. Ruth came out with sheets and pillows and blankets and we made up the sofa and talked for a while.

"Anne, the Library Board is meeting in January, and I will need to offer my resignation. Please plan to be there because I am recommending you as my replacement as Head Librarian. I am sure you'll be offered the job, and I can't think of anyone else who would be better at it. I am going to ask to stay on until at least the start of April."

"Ruth, thank you. I can certainly hold your place until you are ready to return to work."

"We'll see. I'm sure I'll be busy with the baby for a few years. It's so strange to think about that. It makes the whole thing real. Also, Anne, you should plan on a brief presentation to the Board about the changes in services we discussed. I think you should showcase your expertise in that way."

"Alright, I'll work on something, but I'm asking you to listen to my presentation first. I might need your help with it, Ruth."

"You have it. Do you need anything else? Fine, good night. Anne. Stay warm and sleep well, and I'll see you in the morning."

She left for her bedroom, and I got into the warm pajamas I brought and made myself comfortable. The sofa was cozy, and the warm fire made me think of my youth. I fell in and out of sleep for a while. Once I remember waking up, thinking I heard someone walk upstairs, and another time I thought I heard two male voices talking and laughing on the second floor. I knew that Terrence's room was there, but Toby and Ruth stayed downstairs in the large bedroom, didn't they? I thought perhaps I was dreaming and went back to sleep thinking about my coming presentation to the Library Board.

Library Board

When Mr. Wilson retired and decided that due to his arthritis, he would no longer be able to conduct business at the Library Board's monthly meetings, he suggested that a woman replace him. That is how Mrs. Wilson became the fourth member of the Board which considered itself quite modern in asking a woman to be a member. Howard Jones, Everstille Bank President; James Smithy, businessman and owner of the Bijou Theater; and Jason Wicks, lawyer, were the other members of the Board. While Library Board membership was mostly honorific, they met the second Tuesday of every month in the back of the library to hear the report from the one person who indisputably knew and understood the Greenwood Library system: Ruth Evans, whose advice they generally took. So, hiring me as the official Head Librarian was ensured.

On that January Tuesday, after everyone was greeted and coffee and cookies (my chocolate chips) were handed around, Howard Jones called the meeting to order. James Smithy read the minutes from November because no meeting was held in December due to the snow storm. Jason Wicks gave a report on the money spent on the new building, and Mrs. Wilson asked if more coffee was required by anyone. (The Board was not quite as forward thinking as they pretended to be.) Under *New Business*, I stood to give my presentation about alterations and adjustments and plans involving the new library. I did quite well.

Then Ruth asked to speak. She stood and handed each Library Board member a letter which she then read:

> Dear Library Board Members,
>
> This letter serves as notice of my resignation as Head Librarian of Everstille's Harrison Greenwood Memorial Library as of Friday, April 16, 1954 due to the impending birth of my baby. I have treasured the years spent at this institution, and want to thank the Library Board for the help they have given me and the trust they have bestowed upon me during my years here.
>
> It is my recommendation that the current Assistant Librarian, Miss Anne Rivens, be hired to replace me. She has worked with me for years and is professional, competent, knowledgeable, and will be an outstanding choice. She has my full and complete support.

Sincerely,

Mrs. Ruth Evans Pinkerton

I looked up at this. Ruth never called herself *Mrs.* or listed her last name as *Pinkerton*. She hadn't changed it as far as I knew. But she read it loudly and clearly, and then waited for reactions. Mrs. Wilson reacted first.

"Why, Ruth, how wonderful for you and Tobias! What an exciting time for you! Congratulations!"

The rest of the Board rose and came to Ruth and shook her hand. They insisted she sit down, and Jason Wicks ran to get her a glass of water although there was a full glass in front of her. After the congratulations were over, everyone sat down again, and Mrs. Wilson smiled as she asked Ruth a question.

"Ruth, when are you expecting the new arrival?"

"Sometime in May. Doctor Grenville gave the date of May 10 or thereabouts, but with a first child, one is never sure."

You could see the abacus movement in all the heads of the Library Board members. They thought for a few seconds and then after clearing his throat several times and taking a sip of his now tepid coffee, Howard Jones spoke first.

"Mrs. Pinkerton, to touch on a rather delicate subject, if you stay in your position until the sixteenth of April, you will be…that is your baby will…I mean, well, it is unusual for women in your condition to work so long into their, um, …well, you will be showing…" and he stopped here while a flush crept up his face, covering his bald spot on the top of his head. I bit the insides of my cheeks so as not to break out in laughter.

Mrs. Wilson stepped in here. "Dear, perhaps for your health and the sake of your baby, you might consider stopping work before the April date. Perhaps February would be more suitable. In fact, given that it is winter, we fully understand if you would prefer to remain at home and Miss Rivens takes over now. What do you think, Miss Rivens?"

I was startled. Ruth and I discussed the possibility that this timeline would come up, and I knew she was prepared to argue the point. I didn't think I would be involved in this, and was not sure I was prepared. I thought quickly about my reply.

"I am certainly not an expert on these matters, but I do think Mrs. Pinkerton is fully capable of continuing on. There are some essential things which need to be completed and which necessitate her guidance, help, and approval, but we were holding off until the Board's decision about the Head Librarian was made. I will do whatever the Board thinks best, with Mrs. Pinkerton's approval, of course."

I turned to Ruth, as did the Board. She looked around and stood up to speak.

"I know that many women who have jobs outside of their homes do not work once they know they are expecting. However, I want the Board to know that I am physically healthy and under Doctor Grenville's care, and the work I do here is not physically demanding. Miss Rivens and I have a professional working relationship as well as a wonderful personal connection, and she has been extraordinarily helpful in the past few months. The reason for remaining is to oversee the final preparations for the opening of the renovated library in late summer. If there is concern about my physical appearance, I will be in my office most of the day, and Miss Rivens and the part-time staff will be able to continue the usual library work in the public areas. There are some vital library concerns about which the new Head Librarian needs to be aware, and I can help make this a smooth transition."

The Board was quiet for a few moments. Then Howard Jones, his flushed face recovered, spoke.

"I think that the Board should go into an executive meeting right now to discuss this. Would you and Miss Rivens mind if we used the back office? We should not be long."

They moved into the empty meeting room, and Ruth and I sat down. Once the door in the back was closed, I looked at her and said, "I hope I didn't say the wrong things. I was not expecting to be called on like that."

"You said the appropriate things. Honestly, I lengthened the date of my expected resignation. I am hoping they will let me work until at least the middle of March. The lesson here, Anne, is to always ask for more than you expect to get."

She smiled, and we began to clean up the cups and glasses while we waited. The leftover cookies were put away, the table wiped clean, and we sat down again. Soon the Board returned. As they did so, Mrs. Wilson smiled at me, and for some reason, that made me feel better. Howard Jones stood to render their decision.

"First, the Board wants to thank you, Mrs. Pinkerton, for the dedication you have shown over the years. We are aware of the importance of this library to our town, and appreciate your hard work and crucial administration throughout the years We also would like to extend our thanks to Miss Rivens and ask that she accept the job of Head Librarian when you resign, and I think we are in agreement that the end of March should give you enough time to complete the work. Will that be suitable for both of you?"

Ruth glanced at me before speaking. "Thank you, Mr. Jones. That is acceptable. Anne and I should be able to complete the work by then," and she turned to me and motioned for me to speak.

"I am also sure we can complete the work by then. I am happy to accept your offer as Head Librarian, and want to publicly thank Mrs. Pinkerton for her mentoring and guidance over the years."

"Then that is what we will all agree to. Miss Rivens, the Board will meet again next month and make you an official offer. Gentlemen, and Mrs. Wilson, is there anything else we need to discuss before ending this meeting?"

There was not. The January Board Meeting ended. We all shook hands, and the men left. Mrs. Wilson held back because she wanted to speak to Ruth.

"Ruth, again, I am delighted for you and your husband. I will be in touch with you in the next few weeks, As a guiding member of the Rachel Circle, I want you to know that it will be our pleasure to hold a baby shower for you as we have for all the young women of our church. Please take care of yourself and good luck."

And when she left, Ruth turned to me and rolled her eyes. We dressed in out coats and hats and wrapped scarves around our necks. Then Ruth and I walked to the door, turned out the lights, and I walked Ruth to her car, holding her arm to ensure her safety. We said our goodnights, and I walked to my car and drove home.

It was about a week later that Mrs. Wilson called me. She asked for my help in planning and organizing what would be a large and lovely (so she assured me) baby shower.

Baby Shower

I have been to several baby showers in my life. There were some high school friends whose weddings and then, surprisingly soon, baby showers I attended. My sister and sisters-in-law had showers held at the old farm. All these parties were small and intimate gatherings where finger food, candy mints, coffee, and cake, were served. There was also the requisite playing of an annoying set of baby shower games. But Ruth's baby shower proved to be different.

Mrs. Wilson cleared a Friday afternoon in mid-April for the use of the church's basement reception area and proceeded with the planning. She assumed that most of the Rachel Circle would be there along with a few of the women in the congregation, and there would be twelve to fifteen in attendance. However, once the news about Ruth's pregnancy worked its way around the town, women, church members or not, called Mrs. Wilson and manipulated invitations.

Mrs. Wilson was upset. There were close to forty women due to attend the shower, and while all the Rachel Circle members were going to be there, each bringing a platter of finger food, the group was too large to play the annoying baby shower games. She called me and discussed this twice, and I finally convinced her that the games were not that important. After all, with all the gifts, there would be little time to spend on any games. She conceded the point, and I sighed with relief.

I was asked to oversee the decorations. That meant I was told what to purchase, which colors to obtain, and when to drop my acquisitions at the church. I went to Mitchell's Emporium to purchase both the decorations and to order the gift I was getting for Ruth's baby. I knew the shower gifts the women would bring would include the usual: small crocheted and embroidered things, bibs, crib blankets, small soft toys, shake rattles, diapers and pins, and bottles of all sorts. I knew that Ruth's sisters had been invited, and while they could not make the lengthy trip on a Friday afternoon, a baby crib and layette set had been sent to the Pinkerton house. The Chicago sisters of Tobias who sent a highchair and a teddy bear, would not be there either. Ruth had these items in the newly cleaned and painted nursery (which used to be the office) next to the downstairs bedroom. When I visited, she happily showed me all the preparations and gifts for the baby.

As far as I knew, no one had ordered the gift I did. I took some of the cash I had been saving to purchase a new sofa and side table, and ordered the *Boodle Buggy,* an amazing invention which turned into a travel bed and a bassinet as well as the lovely carriage. I was thrilled with the purchase. Ruth and her baby deserved it for all she had done for me since I was eleven, and as soon as the buggy came in and I picked it up, I could not wait for the shower. I took it directly to her house one day after work. Ruth and I admired it and played with it, turning it from a buggy to the bed to the bassinet. It was an amazing object.

The end of March had come, and Ruth had officially resigned from work and would remain at home awaiting the baby's birth. Her final day at the library was a sad one. Many of the patrons came in to say good-bye and wish her well. The Library Board sent over a large decorated cake from Peterson's Bakery, and I cut pieces up and set them around for the visitors. I wrapped a large portion of the cake for Ruth to take home for Toby and Terrence, and the two of us shed a few tears when it was time for her to leave the place she had treasured and built over the years.

The Friday of the baby shower arrived. I closed the library at noon and drove to the church to do my decorating. By twelve-fifteen, the parking lot was half-filled with cars although the shower was not scheduled until two o'clock. The Ruth Circle was there in full force with Mrs. Wilson yelling directions to all the women who were mostly ignoring her. They had set up and decorated for many wedding and baby showers and knew what to do. When I walked in and hung up my coat and hat, Mrs. Wilson glanced at me and immediately turned her head quizzically to the side.

"Hello, Anne. So glad you are here. Where is your apron? Is it in your car?"

I saw that all the women had on various colors of frilly organza aprons, totally useless and, if any food did spill on them, utterly impossible to clean. During her phone calls, Mrs. Wilson reminded me to bring my "best dress apron for the shower". I had no aprons at all. I especially had no frilly organza aprons, and on the rare times I did bake or cook, I wrapped a dishtowel around my waist, or threw one over my shoulder, or stuck one in my waistband. I just looked at Mrs. Wilson and shrugged.

"Well, it's lucky I brought an extra one. Now, come over here and let me tie it on you. Turn around."

She reached over to the corner and pulled out a pink apron, complete with a frilly pocket into which nothing of any purpose could be placed. I turned around and allowed the thing to be tied on me.

"There you go," and Mrs. Wilson patted my shoulders and turned me around, "You look just like one of the Rachels now. Why don't you go over to Mrs. Clampet and see if she needs any help with the food trays? I think the decorations are all in place, and don't they look attractive?"

I turned and looked at the green, yellow, and white streamers falling from the ceiling and surrounding the chair upon which Ruth, honored guest, would sit. The crepe paper from the Emporium had been used to cover and stream and wave throughout the church basement. A large paper stork was taped to the wall behind Ruth's chair. Two paper diapers, one pink and another blue were placed in the stork's beak and a large question mark was pasted onto them. I assumed this was a leftover decoration from other Rachel Circle baby celebrations because I had not gotten them from the Emporium. Had Ruth been there, she would have rolled her eyes at me, and we would have snickered together.

When I found Mrs. Clampet and asked if I could help, she said it had all been done. She sent me to see if the women setting up chairs and tables needed help, and I wandered over to them. I ended up helping to set up folding chairs, a necessary although unappealing activity.

The women began to crowd in by 1:30, carrying wrapped gifts and putting them on the yellow and green crepe paper festooned long table placed in the corner next to Ruth's chair. By the appointed time, Ruth was there and ushered into the food line as the Rachel Circle crowded around her asking her continually how she felt and what they could bring to her. When she sat down holding a teacup and a plate filled with finger sandwiches and yellow and green mints, I came over to sit beside her and held her teacup while she spread a napkin on her lap and set the plate down. Ruth looked pale and her coloring was not what I expected.

She glanced at me and said, "Nice apron!"

"Yes, well, when in Rome…and wait until you see the headgear created for you. You will certainly look like a lady with a paper hat!" I joked. "Ruth, are you feeling alright?"

"I am just a bit tired. My ankles are swollen, and there are pains in my side, but Doctor Grenville said it was nothing to worry about. Please, help yourself to some of this because I don't think I can get any of it down," and Ruth pointed to the overfilled plate. She took the teacup and sipped. Even had she shown any appetite, she couldn't have gotten many bites in because women continually came over to greet her and ask how she was feeling. Finally, she asked me to take the plate back to the kitchen and refill her teacup.

As I did, Mrs. Wilson saw me and said, "Oh, there you are, Anne. I think we should begin to open the gifts now because there are so many. Do you think you can manage to keep track of who gave what? There is a yellow pad and a pencil in the kitchen on the back counter. I am going to make a brief speech and get everyone settled."

I nodded, and she walked away. As I put down the plate and grabbed the pad and pencil, I heard her demand everyone's attention and begin what was not a particularly brief speech about motherhood, and the joys of it, followed by a number of anecdotes about her own experiences with her children. Then she finally remembered to mention Ruth.

By the time I wandered out to the hall, the gifts were being handed around and the usual procedure followed. That involved Ruth, wearing the silly paper hat, opening the gift, reading the card, announcing the giver, and holding up the gift which was greeted by a round of *Oohs* and *Ahhs*. My assigned job was to write down the gift and giver, and by the time the first few gifts has been opened, I looked at the pile left and thought we would not be done by the time of the baby's birth, so I leaned down and whispered to Ruth.

She called Mrs. Wilson over and made a suggestion, and the Rachel Circle began to speed up the procedure by opening the gifts and announcing them. This assembly-line process still took an hour, and I eventually just stopped trying to write it all down. It was four o'clock by the time all the gifts were opened, and the four-thirty children's choir practice would soon begin. Everyone helped clean and clear the basement, and I took many trips to load the gifts into my car. Toby had taken his lunch break to drive Ruth to the church, and I was going to take her and the gifts home. Once the good-byes and thanks were completed, we piled into my car with Ruth holding the remains of the wrapped finger food and cake. I drove her home.

Neither Toby nor Terrence was home yet, so I helped Ruth get into the house and made her sit down while I made numerous trips once again to empty the car. I placed the boxes and bags in the corner of the parlor where they took up quite a bit of space, and when finished, I sat down in the chair across from her and sighed.

I glanced over at the pile and then down at the yellow paper I was clutching which had only a dozen or so names and gifts listed. "Ruth, we will need to go through these gifts again. I didn't do a very meticulous job of notetaking. Sorry."

She laughed. "That's fine, Anne, and I am grateful for your help.

When Toby and Terrence come home, they can help me do that. They will want to look through everything anyway, and we can do that this evening after we eat. I am not sure how many shake-rattles a baby needs, but I stopped the count at five. Why don't you stay for supper? Terrence is going to Mazie's to pick up a dinner, and I can telephone his office and ask him to get extra."

"Thanks, Ruth, but maybe another time. I need to get home and do a few things. I am opening the library early tomorrow morning and then tomorrow night I told Mother I would be over to spend some time with her and Dad. Is there anything I can get you before I leave?"

"No, thanks, I am just going to rest here and hope my swollen feet reduce in size. Terrence will be here in about an hour. Anne, if you are not busy on Sunday, will you come here after church? I have invited Doctor Grenville and his wife for Sunday dinner and would like you to be here too. I want to show the doctor the completed birthing room. He is not so sure I should remain at home for the birth, and I don't want to go to the hospital, so I will try to convince him by showing what I have ready. I don't think we will be at church Sunday, but come right after and we may have a few minutes to talk. Will you?"

"Of course, I will. What can I bring? You know my expertise is limited. Would you prefer the orange Jell-O or some cookies?"

Ruth laughed. "Why don't you just bring yourself? Terrence, our chef, has dinner planned. "

I nodded and got up to hug Ruth before I left. "Fine. Call if you change your mind about the Jell-O, and I'll see you Sunday."

Sunday

Sunday came. The morning was such a perfect spring day that I decided to go for a long walk on Smokehouse Road. My parents sold their buildings and all the land to the Goodwin Company, and I wanted to look at what used to be our farm. I skipped church but would be back in plenty of time to clean-up and dress for dinner at the Pinkerton's.

I started to walk west on Main Street and soon came to the curved road that led down to what used to be the shack where my great-uncles Jake and Lem lived. It had been a while since I had visited. Down the path were two houses, one finished and the other one still being built. The long row of trees, including the oak tree I used to climb into to read, was gone, replaced by small evergreens. I did not walk any closer to the houses, but watched as two young children ran out and slammed the front door and chased around to the back. They stopped when they saw me, and when I waved, they waved back. I walked back down the path and looked up the road to where my parents' farm and house had been. An additional new house and two partly built houses covered the area where I used to run and play with Josh. I wondered if my parents had been out here lately and hoped they had not. I thought this would just make them sad.

I continued to walk west and passed the area of the Martin's farm and the Jasper house, now, both gone. The array of new homes eased back into the area where woods once stood, and I paused and looked, remembering my youthful times. I thought I might walk up to where the narrow paths cut into North Cemetery, but when I glanced at my wrist, I realized I had been gone longer than I thought and needed to get back. *A bit morbid, going to the cemetery,* I thought, not knowing then how soon I would make a trip there.

When I drove up to Ruth's house, I saw that Luke Grenville and his wife, Kat, were there. They had pulled into the long driveway and were getting out of the car. Kat was carrying an enormous bunch of daisies, and I felt bad that I had not thought to bring anything. Not even a Jell-O mold. I waved to them in greeting, and they waited for me to join them. We walked up the front steps to the open front door together.

Toby was standing at the door with Ruth. We greeted each other and the doctor said, "Well, here are the expectant parents. You look well Toby, and Ruth, glad to see you have some color in your cheeks."

I glanced at Ruth and saw there was a flush of red. *At least she looks better than she did Friday*, I thought. We went in and hung up our coats and hats, and Kat gave the flowers to Ruth who went into the kitchen to put them in a vase. We followed and found her arranging the flowers, while Terrence was bent over the oven checking the roast. Everyone greeted him, and Ruth took the flowers out to the dining room table.

When she came back, she spoke, "I'd like to show you the nursery we've decorated. Come and look. I think we're prepared for the baby."

Luke and Kat Grenville and I followed her to the room next to the downstairs bedroom and crowded in. The walls were painted a gentle green, and there were simple but fresh, new white curtains garlanding the window. Kat and I looked around at the zoo of stuffed animals and simple toys arranged on the crib and the bassinet and in the Boodles Buggy which was cushioned against one corner. We admired the paintings of ducks and toys hung on the walls, and pointed out the stack of fresh and ready diapers on top of the new white changing dresser. Doctor Grenville looked on from the doorway and watched us.

"Luke," said Kat to her husband, "isn't this room darling? We'll need to take some decorating tips from Ruth when we have our children. Ruth, this is such a sweet room. What will go over there?" and she pointed to the only empty space.

"Terrence ordered a special rocking chair from the Emporium, but it hasn't come yet. I think it will be in this week, and that's where it will go. I think I'll place this small table to the side of it," and she motioned to the table.

"What a nice gesture. He'll be a wonderful cousin to the baby!" said Kat, and I noted a strained look on Ruth's face. She moved out of the nursery and asked us to follow her to the birthing room.

We walked through the kitchen where Terrence was finishing up the meal. "We'll eat in about five minutes," he warned, and Ruth nodded. Toby followed as we all went to the door next to the pantry, and as Ruth opened it up, we all stepped in.

"Here, Doctor, what do you think? Will this do?"

Luke Grenville stepped into the room and looked around. Since I had seen it, the room was completely cleaned, painted, and carefully organized. The double bed was placed in the middle against the long wall, and the small table and chair were set against the east wall. In the corner was a desk and chair, and another chair was placed next to the bed. Everything was spotless and ready for anticipated activity. Ruth looked at the doctor and waited for a comment.

"Ruth, the room is certainly large enough and close to the kitchen and not far from the bathroom, and I can tell you have put a lot of thought into the decorating of it. As a birthing room, it is sufficient, but I think you and Toby and I should talk later. There are some concerns I need to address with the two of you, but my comments can wait. I smell a delicious dinner," and just at this time, we heard Terrence call, "Dinner is ready."

I could tell that Ruth was not happy with the doctor's pronouncement. Her green eyes flashed, and she looked sideways at me and set her lips in a manner with which I was familiar. She had her stubborn face on, and I did not want to be around when this conversation was held. We left the room, and Ruth closed the door, and we all went to the dining room to eat what was a tasty meal.

While we ate, I talked about my morning walk and the changes that had taken place at our family farm. I told the story of my great-uncles and their shack and the cows that decorated their rooms. The discussion was as lively as the meal was delicious, and when the coffee and Peterson's Bakery pie were served, we sat back and enjoyed dessert. Ruth probably should not have brought up any discussion at the table, especially when Kat and I were there, but she was never one to hold back her thoughts. As we were finished with the meal, Kat and I insisted on clearing the table and doing the dishes. Ruth began to talk.

"Luke, I know we need to discuss some things, and now is as good a time as any. What issues would there be with my having this baby here at home? You know that half of the women having babies in this town do so in their own homes. I was born at home like all my sisters and brother, and Mother had a midwife in attendance. Weren't you and your sister also born at home? So were Toby and Terrence. You know that plenty of women around here and most of the women out on the farms still have home-births."

Doctor Grenville looked around, and although Kat and I could hear perfectly well in the kitchen, we pretended not to and continued a quiet conversation about nothing in particular as we wrapped and put away the leftovers. We began to wash and dry the dishes and stacked the clean ones on the counter.

"Ruth, perhaps this is a discussion you, and Toby, and I can have at another time."

"No time like the present, and Terrence is welcome to stay. He lives in this house, and the baby's birth concerns us all. Is there some reason I should not have the baby here?"

Doctor Grenville looked around, and since Toby was looking expectantly at him, and Terrence showed no signs of leaving, he decided that if Ruth wanted to discuss this now, then he would.

"Ruth, I have delivered babies at home for a number of women in this town. However, and this may be harsh, but the truth is, all were much younger than you, and for most of them, it was not the first birth. I am concerned about your age and the fact that this is your first child."

Ruth looked down and then at the doctor. "Yes, I'm now forty, but that is not too old for a baby. I have felt well most of the time and now that I am not working at the library, I have been watching my diet, and resting, and taking short walks just as you instructed. My age should not be that big a factor."

"No, but it does have some consequences when there is a first birth. Toby, I am sure you and Ruth have discussed this. What is your opinion?"

Toby looked around the table. "I want Ruth to be safe and the baby healthy, Luke. I am willing to go along with whatever Ruth wants as long as she and the baby are protected. But, Ruth, while I don't know much about these things, I do know pain is part of it. Wouldn't there be some help for the pain in a hospital setting?"

The doctor spoke up. "Yes, there are some advantages to being in a hospital. There is *Twilight Sleep* that can be administered to help with the pain, Ruth. Special doctors administer it, and women say they do not feel a thing. They simply are given the drug and wake up a few hours later with their new baby. Why suffer? There are new medicines that can alleviate most if not all of the pain."

Ruth sat for a minute and then got up from the table, walked into her bedroom and brought out some papers.

"That may be, but there are other problems. I have done some research, and *Twilight Sleep* can cause hallucinations and possible breathing problems, and women are strapped down with restraints during the process which does have its drawbacks. Going to a hospital is not one hundred percent safe, and, Luke, I want to be awake and aware when my son or daughter is born. I know there is pain involved, but I feel strong and able. Look at these articles. What do you think?"

The doctor took the papers and glanced through them. He read for a few minutes, then sighed, and passed them back to Ruth.

"Yes, there are restraints involved, but they are for the safety of the woman, and if something unusual was to happen, not that it often does, then the hospital and staff are there to assist. I understand your concern, and I promise you that I will do additional research into this. The next time I see you is Thursday afternoon. Why don't you and Toby come and we can discuss it further?"

Ruth looked at the doctor. Then she looked around at Toby and Terrence. Both were sitting quietly and Terrence had his head lowered. I was peeking out from the kitchen and could tell he was chewing the side of his lip, not a good sign. She nodded and decided not to continue the subject.

"Fine, Luke, we'll talk further on Thursday. Please consider what I want to do. I have thought carefully about this. Now, would anyone like more coffee?" She got up, leaving the papers on the table in front of her and came into the kitchen to get the coffeepot.

Birthing talk was suspended, and the remainder of the afternoon went smoothly. When another hour or so passed, the Grenvilles decided it was time to leave. After the good-byes, Ruth and I moved to the kitchen to finish putting the dishes away, while Toby and Terrence went out to the back porch to enjoy the late afternoon brightness.

"Ruth, I didn't mean to eavesdrop, but of course, I heard the conversation you were having. I don't know much about these things, and I agree with Toby and just want you and the baby to be safe. Maybe Luke Grenville is right. I know that Josh's wife had her last baby in the hospital, and she said it was much easier than the first. She didn't remember a thing, and then it was just like Luke said; she woke up, the baby was there, and about five days later, they both came home. I just don't want you to suffer, and if this *Twilight Sleep* will prevent it, why not take advantage of it?"

Ruth smiled as she handed me the last of the plates to store in the cabinet.

"I want to remember, Anne. Despite the pain involved, I want to have the memory of bringing what will probably be my only child into the world. I want to be here, in the house I have grown to love, and in the room that Toby and Terrence and I cleaned and painted and decorated. I want my son or daughter to spend his or her first night in the nursery with all the toys, and I want to sit in the new rocking chair and hold the baby if he or she cries. I don't want to wait a week to do that. That may sound selfish or silly, but that is what I want. Anyway, I promise I will listen to Luke. We'll talk more about it all on Thursday. I have about a month left, and I have always been in good health, so I'm not too worried about my age. Let's stop this talk and discuss the library conference you are going to attend."

We went to the parlor and continued to talk about library concerns. There was a yearly librarians' conference held in South Bend, and while Ruth usually attended during the week in June, I would be going this year. She explained what I should look and listen for, told me what to expect, and where to eat my meals. She reminisced about her past conferences and said that she would miss going this year. We spent the remainder of the afternoon talking, but when I noted the dusk moving in, I got up to leave. I yelled good-bye to Toby and Terrence who were still on the back porch and turned to hug Ruth. I felt her baby belly as we hugged and told her I would see her soon.

But the following weeks would prove to be busy for many reasons. The work at the library was more demanding than I expected it to be, and consequently, I would not see Ruth too many times during that month. Had I known what was to come, what the future would be, what fate had in store for all of us, I would have made daily trips to the large Victorian house where Ruth and the birthing room both awaited the arrival of the new baby.

New Baby

In 1954, the average age for first-time mothers was twenty-four. The percentage of first-time mothers who were age forty was 1.1%. Total maternal childbirth deaths from pregnancy complications were 5.2% of the total population, and for white women the percentage was 2.1%. Two percent of white females between the ages of 35 and 44 died. Most women gave birth at home in 1900, but by 1938 only fifty percent delivered at home and by 1954-5, the percentage dropped to about one percent. Of those babies whose mothers delivered at home, 89.8% lived when attended by a doctor, and there were 4,078,000 live births in the United States in 1954.

I looked up the statistics a few years after Ruth gave birth to her baby. She was a first-time mother at age forty. Reading through the data, I decided everything seemed to be in her favor. She appeared to be in decent health up to the last weeks of the pregnancy, but apparently there had been a change in her body. Feasibly more than one. Possibly her age had something to do with it. Maybe her blood pressure became elevated. Perhaps her heartbeat was irregular. There might have been some unusual bleeding. There definitely were pains in her abdomen and rib area and major swelling of her feet and legs. Sharp headaches and sleepless nights arrived. But she insisted all was fine, and these were normal pregnancy issues, and for a while, it seemed to be so.

She was resolute about giving birth at home. Luke Grenville had finally agreed with her stratagem, but stipulated that he would immediately move her to the hospital if there appeared to be any unusual problems whatsoever, and Ruth conceded this point. Dr. Grenville discussed the arrangements with Toby who agreed with him. The birthing room was ready. It was immaculate and secure. And, on that Friday morning, when she was certain she was in early labor, it seemed that things would proceed at the typical rate and in the usual way. She called Doctor Grenville when pains began, but they were intermittent. He told her to call when the pains were regular and closer together, or if she felt ill, or seemed to have a fever. She assured him all was well, and she was fine, but late that evening or maybe it was early the next morning, something changed. I was never exactly sure what it was that happened, and I don't believe Toby or Terrence understood how circumstances changed or what had taken place. What awful, dreadful, calamitous thing had occurred.

Late Friday night, she lay in the bed in the birthing room. From what I was told later, she was in a great deal of pain, and there was some bleeding that was not expected. She complained about her swollen legs, and seemed to gain a fever as the night progressed. Doctor Grenville was called and came to the house Saturday morning when the sky was just beginning to be light. He examined her and turned to Toby and said, "I am calling the hospital now. Get some towels into the car, and I will help get her into the back seat."

Toby got the car ready, and he and Luke Grenville carried Ruth to the back seat where Toby stayed, trying to make her comfortable, attempting to reassure her. Terrence drove the car quickly as he followed the doctor's car. There was not much traffic, and later I discovered that Sheriff Samms led the way to Elkhart General, the closest hospital, in his police car, flashing the lights all the way. Once they were there, and Ruth was placed in a room, Terrence called me.

"Terrence, is she alright? What happened? Should I come there? Will the baby be fine?" I didn't know what exactly to ask, and felt helpless.

"No, don't come yet. I'll call just as soon as I know something specific or you are needed. She looks bad, Anne, and is in pain, and there was so much blood. Luke and another doctor are with her now, and Toby and I were asked to leave her room. He is calling the school and making plans for someone to take his place this weekend. I promise, I'll call you as soon as I know anything else."

I knew that the baby was overdue. Ruth had hoped the birth would be over before this weekend which was the annual Spring Festival. This was a yearly event, and many festivities were planned. Toby oversaw the high school activities, but I knew he would not be there this weekend. The town businesses closed early, as did the library. I did not go to the parade or any of the other events. I waited at home by the telephone and paced, waiting for it to ring. Finally, late that night, I fell into a restless sleep only to be awaken early Sunday morning by the jangling telephone. I yanked the receiver up and spoke loudly into it. "Yes? Hello?"

Terrence was on the line. "Anne, it's me. Ruth had the baby late Saturday night, but I didn't want to call you in the middle of the night. She had a difficult time, and neither Toby nor I have been allowed to see her. She's still in bad shape, although Luke told us there are great doctors here, and they're doing the best they can for her. We've been here all night, and I want Toby to go home and get some rest, but he won't leave. Frankly neither of us want to leave."

"Should I come up there? Could I?"

"No, Anne, there is no reason to right now. Ruth is resting and there are lots of nurses and doctors around, so you can't get in. The baby is fine, and apparently Ruth is sleeping on and off. I'll call again in a while if I find anything out. Are you O.K.?"

"Terrence, I'm fine. Please call as soon as you find out something. I will be here all day. I'm not going to church or anything else. Tell Toby not to worry about things here. His assistant principal and the faculty are taking care of it all. They called me last night when there was no answer at your house."

"Thanks, Anne. When I learn something, I'll call. Promise I'll talk to you later."

When we hung up, I realized that I never asked whether Ruth had a son or daughter. Next time he called I would. But Terrence didn't call again until late Sunday night. He sounded exhausted, and his voice was hoarse as if he'd been crying. That upset me. And the news was not good. Ruth was running a high fever. There continued to be bleeding, and Toby could see her only briefly. I knew this particularly upset Terrence, but we both knew the rules, and Toby was her husband. Terrence did not know exactly what the problem was, but he said he would call if there was a change. I told him to call anytime, even during the night. I spent the remainder of the evening on the telephone answering the inquiries of various school faculty and neighbors. I felt stupid because again, I forgot to ask about the gender of the baby, and could only tell those who called that the baby had arrived and seemed to be fine.

Late Sunday night, I took a quick shower and laid out clean clothes for the morning. I decided I was going to go to the hospital, and it did not matter if I couldn't get to see Ruth. I just needed to be there, close to her. Just in case. I called and made arrangements for my assistant librarian to open the library Monday, gave her some directions, and then I tried to get some sleep.

It was a few minutes after six in the morning and the phone rang. It was Terrence.

"Ruth is asking to see you, Anne. Can you get here quickly? Just be careful driving. Luke Grenville said he would leave a special pass for you at the main desk so that you could get up to the room. Anne, I'm really worried. Ruth is bad off, and I'm not sure…" and he could not finish as his voice broke.

"I'm on my way."

I threw on my clothes and left, rushed to my car, and started off towards the hospital. I was stunned. I tried not to cry, but tears blinded me in the half light, and once I had to pull over on Smokehouse Road to wipe my eyes and collect myself. I took some deep breathes and drove as quickly as I could. When I arrived at the hospital, I parked and ran into the building to the main desk. I took the elevator to the third floor and showed my pass to the nurse at the desk who pointed to room 312.

I went into the room. The nurse was removing a bundle from Ruth's arms, and as she walked out of the room, I gave a passing glance to her newly-born daughter who was wrapped snugly in a pink receiving blanket. The child was transported into the nursery, being removed from sight since she was deemed both a joy and an offence to her dying mother. I looked at the bed and thought, *I have come too late*, but then Ruth opened her eyes, still green although they were faded, and looked at me.

"Come here," she whispered hoarsely, and I moved to her right side and knelt by the bed. She opened her hand to me. I took her right hand and brought it to my lips, all the while watching her face, watching the paleness, hoping for a sudden change, for a healthy blush to cover it. Ruth smiled weakly. I knew it was a farewell.

Toby was sitting at her left side. His head was bowed, and he slumped in the chair. He held Ruth's left hand in both of his, softly caressing it. Standing behind him was Terrence whose hands were on Toby's shoulders. I thought about the tableau we created and realized that the four of us were connected physically. We held on to each other and to Ruth as though touching her, gripping her actual flesh, would keep her soul anchored to it.

She closed her eyes, and we stayed there, barely breathing ourselves, not speaking because all the words had been said. Simply waiting, watching Ruth diminish. We were an assemblage of statuary, frozen in place, immobile, inactive, inert, as the early sun, moving up slowly from the horizon, lit the room, creating a backdrop for our gloom.

A nurse came in to examine Ruth. She checked her and the machines, then left; and in a little while, Luke Grenville came into the room. He quietly greeted us and went to Ruth who lay still although she still breathed. He examined her pulse and felt her head. He scrutinized the wires and instruments to which she was attached and looked sad. He stood for a moment, then squeezed Toby's arm as he left. There was nothing to do now. Nothing except wait for the inevitable.

Suddenly Ruth opened her eyes. She took a breath, and then let it out slowly, weakly, pressing my hand. She turned her head to her husband, to Toby, giving him a slight smile. I hope he saw because his head was bowed, and water trickled from his blue Aegean Sea eyes. I watched as Ruth lifted her face, past Toby, up to Terrence, bequeathing her final mortal gaze to the face of the Chicago cousin we both had known for years was no kin to Toby. As her green eyes glazed over, they did not leave the face of Terrence Douglas, and his eyes, his blue/green/gray eyes, crowded with tears as Ruth ceased her breathing, and the wetness quietly fell down his face, left his cheeks, and gently showered the flaxen locks which curled on the head of Tobias Pinkerton.

Ruth's Funeral

I do not know who started it. Nor do I know how the news spread. I know I did not get a phone call or a message, and perhaps because I was working alone in the shuttered library while the new one was being completed, and the library books were being moved, I was out of the loop. However, during the three days of the Ruth's wake and funeral, hundreds of books, maybe a thousand, maybe more, were left, piled up around her casket, creating tangible offerings to her. I haven't counted them or catalogued them all yet. It will take weeks.

Jamison's Funeral and Livery Services had morphed into Jamison's Funeral Home Services, opening in a brand-new building containing spacious viewing rooms. Ruth was waked there on Thursday and Friday, and her funeral was Saturday. I went to work at the library Thursday morning just to keep myself occupied. Then at noon, I went home to clean up and put on my black dress. Since I only had one, I would wear it for the three days with different sweaters and jewelry and scarves, and make it look like three new outfits. At least that is what I read in the article from one of the new women's magazine Ruth had ordered for the library. I heated up some soup, but could not get down more than a few bites, so I washed the dishes and started out for Jamison's.

Toby and Terrence told me I should be there at two o'clock with them and the rest of the family, but I felt strange about doing that. I thought if I got there a little later there would not be too many visitors and I could slip in. When I got to Jamison's, I was surprised to see the parking lot was full, and there were people milling about outside. I opened the heavy oak door and found the room whose sign announced: **Ruth Evans Pinkerton**, and stopped in total surprise. It was not the sight of my friend and mentor lying in a casket covered with beautiful flowers that struck me. It was the books. There were already stacks of books piled up around the casket.

I found Toby and waited until he saw me. Then I went over and hugged him. He held me and gave a sob, and after a while pulled back and wiped his eyes. I pointed to the books and watched as additional townspeople came in, almost all of them holding a book, sometimes two, and a few, three.

"I know," said Tobias in answer to my gesture. "Ruth had quite an influence on the town. People started bringing in copies of books, books she had suggested they read, books which turned out to be favorites. Some are library books she told them to keep and reread. Mr. Jamison said books began to be dropped off to his office over the past days, and he stacked them up. They keep coming in. I guess it's a true tribute to Ruth, and she would have loved it."

"I didn't know about this. But I'll bring one in tomorrow. Not sure what will happen to these, but you are right, Ruth would love it. Where is Terrence?"

"He's staying with the baby until the nurse we hired to watch her gets to the house. We brought her home with us since she is healthy. Neither of us could imagine her being alone in the hospital and wanted her in her own room, in her own crib. Terrence should be here soon."

"I'll look for him. I think I want to examine the books," and I squeezed Toby's hand and walked over to the first stack.

The book on top was Steinbeck's *The Grapes of Wrath,* and the one underneath was Willa Cather's *O Pioneer!,* and I smiled at that one. New copies of *The Little Prince* and *Catcher in the Rye* and *Animal Farm* lay there. There were plays by G.B. Shaw and mysteries by Agatha Christie. Children's books were in the stacks, and I saw quite a few of the Andrew Lang fairy books, and Mark Twain's *Huckleberry Finn,* and Lewis Carroll's Alice books. There were some books on science and philosophy and religions, and some were new and others well-loved and well-read. I did not want to move the stacks, but I thought I would begin to count them. I gave up because as the night progressed, more and more books arrived. The first night ended, and I went home exhausted. Before I went to bed, I looked through my library of books and found the one I would bring with me the next day.

The following day, I did not go to work. I stayed in bed later than usual, and when I got up, I did some straightening and cleaning just to pass the time. When I was ready, in my same black dress, draped with a multi-colored scarf and carrying a different sweater than yesterday, I went to Jamison's. There were people there even though it was barely three o'clock, and the viewing had just started. Almost everyone held a book. I walked in with a group and watched as they walked to Ruth to say their good-byes and placed their book or books on the growing stacks. Toby and Terrence were both there, standing at the front, greeting neighbors and friends and strangers they did not know, but apparently Ruth had.

I waited until there was a lull, and then went to Ruth. I spoke the words to her that I needed to, and then I wiped my eyes and kissed the book in my hands. I did not place it on a stack but set it on the top of the flowers which adorned her casket. The book settled in. I offered my copy of Dicken's *Oliver Twist*, the first book Ruth had assigned me, the book she had me read, the one that began our discussion on good and evil. This was the book which, when I finished, Ruth asked: *Does it tell a good story? If you can answer in the affirmative, then your time has not been wasted. A good story is the first rule.*

Those three days were trying and wretched. The funeral at the church was fully attended, and there was an overflow crowd standing in the vestibule. When Toby saw me, he took my arm and moved me into the front pew with the families. I don't remember much of that day except for the grief and the tears. I do remember thinking that I had not seen the baby yet. She was being cared for at home by a nurse, and I was looking forward to meeting her and seeing the small person who had taken Ruth's place. I could not hate her. She was part of Ruth, and I had made certain promises I was going to keep. I wanted to spend time with her, wanted to get to know her, wanted to see if her mother's intelligence was in her eyes, wanted to call her by her name. She was Olivia Anne.

***

The new library was built, and while the finishing touches were being put on it, I had some free time. There were many things to do as the new Head Librarian, but most of them needed to wait until I hired and trained additional staff. Toby had decided to donate all the books given at Ruth's wake to the library. They would be housed in a new room called the *Ruth Evans Pinkerton Room*. Special dedication labels had been ordered and would be placed in all the books which would come to be known as *Ruth Books*.

I was taking advantage of the library's closure. The week following Ruth's funeral, I attended the special five-day class/seminar given for librarians at South Bend's Indiana University, just as Ruth suggested. I thought it would be a good break for me after all the sadness, and I was excited about being in a college setting. I decided to travel there a couple days early, and I stayed a couple days later, taking a vacation, something I had never done.

Once I returned home and reorganized and went back to work, I telephoned Toby. We spoke for a while, and I asked about Terrence and how Olivia Anne was doing.

"We are all fine, Anne. We are figuring it out and have plenty of help with Olivia Anne, but it is difficult without Ruth. I miss her. We miss her. I continually blame myself for not insisting she have the baby in the hospital. I think about it every day."

"Toby, you know how she felt and what she wanted. She was so healthy through most of the pregnancy and was positive there wouldn't be any problems. You can't blame yourself. Please don't."

We spoke for a while longer and I made plans to come over Saturday and spend the afternoon with them. It had been almost a month, and I had only glimpsed Ruth's daughter. I wanted to see her, and hold her, and remember my friend.

I was not scheduled to work Saturday which turned out to be lovely, so I walked to Ruth's house, and took my time. I walked down Main Street, stopping at Peterson's Bakery to pick up some of their famous donuts and continued my stroll with the sun shining on my face. I went up the steps to the old Victorian house and was greeted by Toby who opened the door for me.

"Good to see you, Anne," and he hugged me. "Come in. Terrence took Olivia Anne out for a short walk around the block in her new buggy. They'll be back in a few minutes. Let's go into the kitchen. Just made some fresh coffee. Umm, must be the donuts."

I noticed that the paraphernalia connected with a baby was all around: blankets and soft toys, bottles, and delicate pink clothing. We sat at the kitchen table and Toby got out three cups and poured the coffee. I put the donuts on a plate, pulled out the creamer from the fridge, and put it next to the sugar bowl. As we sat down, we heard Terrence.

"Hello! We're back. She liked being outside, but I covered her up completely so no wind would blow in her face. The buggy is a nice one, Anne. You need to take her out for a walk in it one of these days."

Terrence came into the kitchen holding the bundled-up baby. He came over to me and placed her into my arms. I choked up as I looked at her. She was lovely. Only a month old, but Olivia Anne looked healthy and happy. As she turned her head, she opened her eyes, and while there was still some blue to them, I could see some gray also, and perhaps some green. She might have her mother's eyes. She still had her bonnet on, and Toby reached over to take it off. He felt under her chin, untied the bow, and carefully removed it. Later, as I walked home, I thought back to this moment, and hoped I did not allow the jolt I felt in my soul to sound out from my mouth. I pray I kept my shock to myself as I realized the last secret I was never told.

Olivia Anne's soft, wispy hair was beginning to cover her head. It was delicate and fluffy, and Toby reached over to brush some of it out of her tiny face. I leaned in to her, partly to take a sniff of her sweet baby smell and partly to cover up the surprise on my face. Olivia Anne's hair was the color of a new copper penny but two shades lighter. It shone like the orangey gold of autumn leaves; it was like the last streak on the horizon when there was an auburn/gingery sky at night. Stripes of gold mixed with flashes of burgundy made it apparent who she was; made it evident to whom she belonged; made it positively clear whose eyes she had.

I said nothing but held and rocked her until she fell asleep. After, I carried her to the nursery, kissed her head, and laid her down, covering her with a delicate pale pink blanket. I said my good-byes. I promised I would telephone in a couple days, and we would make plans for me to come over and take her for a stroll in the buggy. I moved down the walk and turned and waved, and watched them both, Toby and Terrence, standing together, shoulder to shoulder, in the doorway of the large Victorian house. I knew they would care for and raise Olivia Anne, Ruth's daughter. Furthermore, I knew I would also be part of her life. Just as I promised Ruth.

Tobias Pinkerton

1. May 22

My Dearest Livie,

It is late, and I am tired, but I wanted to get this started. I am not sure if I will write daily. I expect not, so this may take a while before it's completed, so I'll number and date these entries as I write. I'm unsure how long this will take, but I want it done and frankly, out of the way. You will not read this for years, but it is important to get it right. Your Aunt Anne (I am sure that by the time you read this, you will know she is not your *aunt*. You will know the truth about all of us.) told me that I owe you this, that I should write down what the truth is because you will want to know it someday. She is right. She is also wise in asking me to give this to her for safekeeping when I finish, for fear I will come to the conclusion that this is a bad idea and destroy it. I will do that also. She is also right that when you are older, all you will need to do is glance in a mirror to discern the truth. Anne is aggravatingly right about most things.

She has also asked your Uncle Terrence (again, you will learn the truth) to write his story, but he has refused. He claims that his writing is not good enough; that he is not sufficiently educated; that he would not know how to start, and his handwriting is terrible. These objections are probably correct because Terrence is not a writer. I don't remember him writing more than a short note or his signature in years. Even at his job, he is a talker and not a writer. I know this because he has always asked for my help when he must turn in a semi-annual report. Terrence would most likely answer questions in person if you have them, if we are still around when you read this, if you are still even having anything to do with us. This worries me, and I considered it when I was deciding whether to write our story. But I think the truth outweighs any lies in this case. So, I will write the truth.

Today is your first birthday. You are asleep in your room, the small office we turned into a nursery which is next to the large bedroom where I sleep. And which Terrence sometimes shares. We have not yet determined what to do about this as you get older. Terrence officially stays in one of the three bedrooms upstairs. His belongings are there, and his shaving and personal effects fill the bathroom down the hallway. You may move upstairs to a room as you get older and demand your own space away from me. That will most likely happen, but for now, you sleep peacefully in your own little nursery where I can check on you during the night as I get up and wander around because I cannot sleep.

Your birthday today was bittersweet. One year ago, two days after you were born, your mother Ruth took her last breath. It was Monday, early morning. You were born late Saturday, after eleven at night, and we still thought and hoped Ruth would survive. She held you briefly, and in her weakened state, kissed you and cried over you. You should know this. Your mother gave you a life-time of love and care in the few hours she held you. All of us were with her as she died. Anne and I were each holding her hands, and Terrence was behind me. I know that because he kept his hands on my shoulders attempting to give me strength.

It was the Saturday of our yearly Everstille Spring Festival celebration. The townspeople were preparing for the big dance held in the high school gym, and normally, I would have been there. I was not. My assistant principal took over my duties while I was with you and Ruth. This weekend was the Festival, and the dance was last night. I went because I felt I should show up this year but stayed for only a brief time. Terrence was here, at home, with you, and fed you dinner, and got you ready for bed. I think it is important that you understand we both care for you. We have hired Sally, to care for you during the day, and as you grow, you will understand all our roles. I think it helps to write some of these words down for myself. There is so much guilt I feel.

Today was Sunday, but we did not attend services at church. We prepared for the small party we gave for your birthday. You even got a piece of the cake, and we all laughed as you ate small bites, getting the yellow frosting on your nose. Aunt Anne took a picture of you between Uncle Terry and me as we smiled into the camera. There were few other guests here for the celebration. Besides the three of us, there was Anne, Anne's mother (her father was ill and could not come), Sally and her husband, all gathered around the dining table. A small party, but then, as I wrote before, a bittersweet time, and a difficult one to celebrate.

Yesterday, Terrence and I took you to the parade downtown. We did not stay long because it was windy, and the noise and crowd scared you. You are starting to talk, and you raised your arms to me and called "DaDa", and I picked you up out of the buggy Aunt Anne gave you and which you are outgrowing. You clung to me, and Terrence held your hand and you called him "Ter" in your new little voice. We had several discussions about what to teach you to call us, and decided on those appellations. We will try to keep it simple, to keep it obvious and forthright. At least for outsiders. Terrence and I know the truth and came to an agreement a long time ago. Before you were even born.

I am getting tired and not sure that what I am writing is even making sense, so I will stop for tonight. This week is the start of summer break, and school is closed until the summer session which begins in a few weeks. I will be home with you throughout this time. Sally will have a break, and I think she is going to visit her daughter in South Bend. Terrence will go to work as usual, and I wonder how you will account for this change. I am looking forward to watching you and playing with you. I will need to go into the school for a few hours each week, but plan on taking you with me. My secretary, Mrs. Green, said she is looking forward to seeing you and can care for you when I have paperwork to complete or a meeting to attend. There are so many people in this town who are willing to watch and care for you. I know it is because they admired Ruth. There is also a suspicious feeling that they also want to get a good look at you, at your eyes, at your hair, but that is to be expected. It is human nature to be curious; it is small-town nature to be nosy.

The moon is bright and almost full tonight, and as I complete this first entry, I see the brightness of it shining outside your window and into your room. The luster of it surrounds your head, and if I listen carefully, you are letting out tiny snoring breaths every now and then. You are such a clever and happy baby. I see your mother's intelligence growing in you daily.

I'll stop now and go to bed. Terrence is upstairs sleeping. He was tired and went to bed since he begins work early tomorrow. I hope to sleep soon, but there have been too many nights in the past year that I have lain awake until dawn reviewing things in my mind, thinking about my life and the errors and sins I have committed. I look at you sleeping the sleep of innocents and want no sleepless nights for you. Ever.

2. June 3

You probably want to know the history of Terrence and me, and I will get to that. You need to know about my background first because I am sure it will help you understand. I was born here, in Everstille. My older sisters, Ernestine, and Gladys, and I grew up in the main town until my parents built a small house out on the old Smokehouse Road. Then we moved there, and I took the school bus into school alongside the farm kids who lived even farther out. I don't remember much until I was older. Junior high years were difficult. I was, for reasons I could not understand then but are perfectly clear to me now, often teased and a few times, set upon by other boys in my class. I did not have many friends, just my sisters. As they grew older and became interested in other things, they stopped playing with me. I spent most of the time by myself or with my mother. Father was busy with his handy-man business, and soon after he retired, he died.

Ernestine married right after high school, and she and her husband, Amos, moved to Chicago where he had the promise of a good job at one of the factories there. After Father died, Mother sold the house to the Jaspers, and we moved to Chicago with Ernestine and Amos who had moved into a large house and were having trouble keeping up the payments. Mother's small inheritance and some money from the sale of the house made it easier for all of us to live together. Once we got settled, Mother found some work as a seamstress and was able to complete her piecework from the house. During high school, I found a part-time job delivering newspapers. Gladys found a job and soon a husband, so once she married and moved out, Mother and I stayed upstairs in the two bedrooms.

School was challenging in Everstille, and I hoped that school in Chicago would be easier. In some ways, it was. I was able to hide in the crowded hallways and classrooms. What saved me from being bullied was my ability to swim. I joined the school swim team and achieved a small measure of popularity. I completed my high school diploma, and then, with the help of a partial scholarship, went to Chicago Normal College where I studied to be a teacher. That is where I met Terrence. We became friends, and eventually I moved back to Everstille, and after a few years, he moved here.

Those are the bare bones of our story. I'll attempt to flesh it out for you, and will be judicious and careful as I write. I may hint at things, but I will not and cannot tell you details. When you read this, you will be wise enough to fill in the blanks. Of that, I am sure.

I need to clarify about the teasing that happened when I was young. I say, without pride, and only as an observation, that I have always been considered an attractive person. My sisters would brush my blonde hair which Mother kept longish when I was young, and talk about how unfair it was that their hair did not have the color and shine mine did. They spent hours looking into Mother's small hand-mirror at their eyes, wishing them the color of mine…*sky-blue* was what they called them, and moaning that their lashes were not as full as mine. It was not fair, they would often tell me, that I was a boy and got all the looks in the family.

This never bothered me, and I never thought anything of it until a new family moved into the town when I was in sixth grade. There was a boy whose name now eludes me, although perhaps I just don't want to remember, who took it upon himself to single me out and call me names. He called me *pretty boy* among others, and would push me whenever he got the chance. He became the ringleader of a group of sixth and some seventh-graders who made the next couple years of my school-life miserable. Now, as an educator, I understand his adolescent behavior. I studied enough psychology to realize what this boy feared. Then, all I could think of was how miserable I was. I did not yet understand my own nature, although I'm sure that even given that knowledge, nothing would have changed. During my eighth-grade year, my father died, and my mother decided to take Gladys and me to Chicago to live with Ernestine and Amos. I was unhappy and distressed about the loss of my father, but I was not unhappy about the eventual decision Mother made about moving to Chicago. I was anxious to start over. I wished to have an easier time of it.

You should understand that I always felt different. I could not discern why I did, but I felt I did not belong anywhere. The small town of Everstille did not then, and still to a great extent, does not now tolerate many differences in their citizens. Everyone is expected to adhere to the traditions and standards and mores of male and female roles. I did not know that when I was twelve, but understand it now. I don't believe my family, especially my parents, noticed any difference in me, and Mother would have been alarmed and offended had she realized certain facts about her only son. I am not sure she ever suspected, and, if she had, I am certain she would have considered me an aberration, a sinner. So, it is better, now that she is gone, that she never knew. My sisters may suspect certain things, but they do not ask, and I do not offer. We are not close, and I don't see them more than once or twice a year.

Given all these expectancies and beliefs, the irony of my moving back to Everstille weighs heavily on my mind. I hope, with the help of Terrence and Anne, that you will grow up accepting and understanding those who, like me, feel they are different. And may very well be so.

3. June 19

I am almost two years younger than Terrence. I just turned eighteen when I began to take classes at Chicago Normal College. Terrence was there taking a few classes and working in the building and on the grounds as a part-time custodian, but we did not know each other until my second year. We had a class together and ended up in the library doing research for it. We reached for the same book, and that is how we met. That may have been the last class he took. Terrence was not interested in a higher education, and the small stipend he had been awarded to assist him was just about gone. He had the job at the college and another at a restaurant/bar on weekends, and when the stipend ran out, he continued those jobs but stopped attending college classes.

It was during the Depression, and money was a problem for everyone. It was not unusual to have, if you were lucky, two jobs and still not be able to make the monthly bills. I was fortunate to have two part-time jobs. I continued my newspaper delivery job (adding sales) for the afternoon edition of the *Chicago Daily News* and happened to meet a reporter who was a great reporter but a poor writer. He paid me to rewrite and edit his stories because he couldn't turn in his badly written notes. He enjoyed the interviewing and the investigating, but hated the actual writing, and paid me to help decipher his annotations. It wasn't a real part-time job because the editing was so intermittent, but I kept that bit of money earned for my writing. I gave most of my other earnings to Mother to help with the expenses at the house. There were four adults, and between us and all the jobs we worked, we were able to survive until times got better.

College work was not difficult for me, and on my street-car rides to the campus in Englewood, I did most of my reading and planning for classes. I wanted to get as much done as possible then because my job was time-consuming, and because I wanted time to be with Terrence. We were able to be together more often when he was working on the campus, but during my last year in college, he decided that spending money on street-cars was a waste, so he quit the college custodial job and went to work full-time at the restaurant/bar where he earned better money and great tips.

A bit about Terrence. You know he is friendly and outgoing. You are aware of his charm and natural intelligence. He has a terrific sense of humor and love of life. Because he is a large, burly man, one who appears tough, most people don't expect him to be kind and understanding, but he is. When I got to know him better, I understood why so many people were attracted to him…both women and men. Working at the restaurant/bar where he did was easy for him because his small apartment was not far from it, and he could walk to work. I rarely saw him during my last year, and frankly, was glad to graduate because that freed me up to spend additional time in his presence. And I found myself wanting to be with him.

I continued my part-time job selling and delivering papers after I graduated because there were few teaching jobs available, even though I had been trained specifically to teach in the Chicago schools. I worked periodically as a substitute teacher and got some practical experience in handling classes, but it was not what I wanted to do which was to teach English literature and writing. As a substitute, I was sent into various classrooms. Sometimes I ended up substituting in elementary schools, and other times I was expected to take over a high school science or math class. I kept introducing myself to the principals of the schools I was sent to in the hopes that something would turn up, and I would be offered a full-time job. And I grew distant from my actual family. By this time, Ernestine had one child and was unable to continue working, so a decision was made to reorganize the household and move Mother downstairs to one of the small bedrooms. Walking the stairs was becoming more difficult for her anyway. Her room was rented out, and the money from the boarder was useful.

I knew that the amount of money I was offering for household expenses would not be as beneficial as obtaining another boarder and renting out my room, so I suggested I move out, telling my family I had a friend who was willing to share his apartment with me. I spoke to Terrence, and that is how I ended up sharing the small rooms with him. I was able to offer him the same amount of money to help pay for our expenses, and he got permission for me to stay with him when he introduced me as his "Chicago cousin" to his landlady, a ruse we continue to this day. Terrence and I lived together and were happy.

Periodically, Terrence would have a girlfriend. I accepted that about him, and he was always honest with me. Every now and then, whatever girl he was seeing would ask if he could find her friend a date, so I sometimes became a companion to her friend, and Terrence and I and went on dates together. A strange situation, but I grew used to it. I never really enjoyed women's company the way Terrence did. At least, not until I met Ruth. In some ways, ours was a strange life. We both worked. And dated women. And, in the small apartment we shared, became something more than roommates. I hope I am not shocking you at this point, Livie, but I suspect that now, as you read this, you understand that human nature is complicated, and there are many kinds of love.

I will stop here for tonight.

4. August 20

This is more difficult than I thought. I have been at this for months, have rewritten practically everything, and do not seem to be very far along in this project. The fall school session is almost here, and I'm busy with meetings and planning. Sally has returned from her vacation, and the first day she was here, and I had to leave for a day of meetings, you cried and called "Dada. Stay!", and my heart broke. But Sally said that as soon as I was out of sight, you turned and took her by the hand to show her your room which Terry repainted a bright yellow. You are currently into all things that color. Fickle child!

You are walking, and each day you get better at it. Terry and I take walks with you up and down our street, and when you trip and fall, you jump up and laugh. Terry laughs too and says, "Look at the little cabbage. She is showing such signs of independence!" I don't know how he knows that. He has had no more dealings with babies than have I. Anne comes here often, and you get excited to see her and go running for a hug. She has recently begun to wear glasses, and you are fascinated with them, so that may be the reason. She lets you put them on, and we laugh at how funny you look. Anne comes here after church on Sundays, and we all spend the day together. When you take your afternoon nap, the three of us sit and discuss the week's activities, argue about politics, gossip about the town, and always end up talking about Ruth.

The last entry ended with a comment about love, and I suppose that is a valid place to continue writing this tale. I must make it clear to you that I have loved many people in many ways. You are my greatest love, and I want you to know that. I loved your mother, Ruth, although not in the way a husband might. She was aware of this, and we came to terms about it. Anne has my love as a friend and because she takes such devoted and benevolent care of you. I love Terrence and have for years. We have disagreed and fought but worked through the issues. He is the one constant in my life after you, and I believe he feels the same. I can mark my feelings for Terrence from the time we lived together in Chicago.

That small apartment we shared was our home. Terry worked evenings and into the early morning hours. Often, he did not get home until it was time for me to get up and get to a school when I had a substituting assignment. In the afternoons, I tended to the newspapers, so we had little time to spend together except for the periodic weekday night. When I got home, about five in the evening, he would be up and ready for work, and have dinner made. Terry worked behind the bar of the restaurant and often in its kitchen and consequently, became a decent cook. You know by now that he does most of the cooking and baking and is excellent at it. Anyway, those dinners were the times we spent together; the few hours when we could talk and laugh and feel like a couple.

Our small boarding house apartment was on the north side of Chicago in an area sometimes called *Towertown*, not far from Washington Square Park, which was the source of diverting activities. People came to the park and voiced their opinions on many subjects as they stood on boxes and gathered a crowd. Musicians and poets performed. Sometimes a band played, and Terry and I, whenever we had a chance, and he had a free night, would walk, and enjoy the crowds, the noise, the amusements. Entertaining clubs and bars were not far, and often we would end up at one of them. On those nights we were able to go and be together, we felt accepted and did not worry about people staring at us if he rumpled my hair or I squeezed his shoulder. There were many couples, both men and women, who walked and felt free and able to be themselves. But society is restrictive, and we were always guarded and careful about our behavior towards each other.

There was a university, more than one, not that far from the park, and students from the schools would come in groups to see what was happening. They had as much a right as anyone else to be there. After all, the place was an area where free speech and rights were celebrated and respected. However, these college students were not always as respectful as they might have been. At times, they would shout down the speakers or harass couples who were not careful about their affections, and one humid, warm summer evening, Terrence and I were there when a couple standing in front of us became the unwanted focus of their interests.

A would-be actor who was costumed in Elizabethan dress had been entertaining the crowd by reciting several Shakespeare's sonnets. He had concluded with the one that begins:

> *A woman's face, with nature's own hand painted,*
> *Hast thou, the master-mistress of my passion;*

And ends:

> *But since she pricked thee out for women's pleasure,*
> *Mine be thy love, and thy love's use their treasure.*

Now, I am assuming that when you read this, you have a passing knowledge of the sonnets and know something about to whom some were allegedly written. I suggest you ask Anne to help you out with this if you need additional knowledge, but the fact is, Terrence and I laughed at it as did much of the crowd. In front of us, one man leaned into his partner's ear and said something I will not write, but was heard by many of us who were gathered there. The remark was personal and meant to be funny, but was not suitable for such a mixed crowd. One of the college students standing close to us heard it and reacted.

"Hey, there's some fruitcakes here!" he yelled and the group pushed us out of the way and surrounded the couple in front of us. The students gathered around and started to laugh and point and call names.

The fact that it was hot and humid with a storm on the horizon, and the group had obviously been drinking did not help the tension. When the first student who called names reached out and swiped his hand across the cheek of one of the men, a wild fight began. Terrence took my arm and pulled me back, and I assumed we were going to leave the premises. But one of the students backed up into me and quickly turned and, without thinking, drew his arm back and hit me in the face. Terry reacted fiercely.

He pulled back and hit the student who touched me and knocked him down. That was the start of the general row. Soon it was difficult to tell who was who. We both took several blows and gave some, and when we heard police sirens, Terry grabbed my arms and pulled me up because I had just been knocked down. Again. He ran, and I followed, and eventually we wound up blocks away where we ducked into an alley and wiped our faces with our, by then, rain-soaked shirts, and tried to look presentable. We walked quickly in the rain, taking over an hour to get back to our apartment. Once inside, we examined the damage done to our persons, cleaned up, and changed our wet clothing. We settled in the small kitchen, Terry made a pot of coffee, and we sat down to drink it and talk about the evening. After a couple of general comments about the mayhem and fight, I asked him about his actions.

"You reacted so quickly when that guy hit me. Why? Didn't you think I could take care of myself?"

He sipped his coffee and looked down at the floor and was silent for a bit. Then he looked up and smiled. "No, I knew you could. Honestly, I didn't even think about it. Once when my little brother, Tommy, was outside, one of the neighborhood kids began to kick him. When I saw it, I yelled, ran over, pushed the kid off and began to go after him. He ran away, and I got Tommy into the apartment where he was safe. I didn't even think about what I did tonight. I just knew that no one was going to hurt someone I felt responsible for. And that is how I felt tonight. Sorry if I stepped in and shouldn't have."

That was the closest Terrence had even gotten to expressing any sentiments for me. In fact, it still is. But I knew, and still do, that the feelings I have are reciprocated. They are expressed in actions, not in words. Maybe that way is the more trustworthy.

There, that is something for you to consider. And now, in both actions and words, I am going to bed. Good-night little Livie.

5. September 9

Cheap living with Terrence and working two jobs allowed me to save some money. I bought an old car and drove it to schools when I had a substitute job. It saved me hours on the crowded, slow street-cars. I also drove it on those Sundays I went to visit Mother at Ernestine's house. At times, Terry was responsible for the Saturday night shift at work and would not return home until early Sunday morning. Because he slept most of the day, I left him alone and used the time to visit my family. Mother was always happy to see me, and when the weather permitted, I took her for a ride in my car.

One such Sunday, after Ernestine served the dinner of meat loaf and mashed potatoes, Amos and I talked on the front steps while my two nephews, Enoch and Otis, chased each other on the front sidewalk, and the women cleaned up. Amos was amiable and I liked him, and because we both came from Everstille, we had that in common. His mother and aunt still lived there, and he would fill me in on the happenings in the town as told to him through his mother's letters.

"I guess the new high school will be opening up in Everstille. They turned that old unused warehouse into a school, and Ma said with all the changes and work, it looks real good and modern."

"Really?" I pretended interest. "That's good. Shows progress. I'm sure they needed a new building."

"Yes, and, say, if you was ever wanting to return, Ma said they couldn't get many new teachers to live in the town and need some to fill in the blanks. Maybe you could teach there. Wouldn't that be something? You returning to a place you left when you was ten!"

"I was twelve, but it doesn't matter. Did your mother say what kind of teachers were needed? What grades or subjects they needed them for?"

"Nope. But you could probably write old man Jenkins. He's still the principal there. Heard his wife died a few years back but he keeps pluggin' along. Hey! Boys! Stop that now!"

Amos got up to break up a fight between his sons, and I sat on the steps and ran the news through my mind. Substituting in the Chicago school system was a thankless, low-paid job. It required me to drive all over the city, and no matter where I went, it did not seem as though

English teachers were wanted permanently. Jobs were precious and people hung on to them. I wanted to teach, and it was difficult to do so now, so I began to consider the possibility of going back to Everstille.

I went home and sat on this information for a while and didn't say anything to Terry. I considered all sides of the issue, and finally, I sent a letter of inquiry to Clarence Jenkins, Everstille's principal. Two weeks later, he replied saying that there would be an opening for an English teacher at the high school in the fall, and he offered me the position. He remembered my parents and sisters and inquired after my family, and I suspect that my being from Everstille was part of the reason for the offer. I guess he figured that I had grown up there, knew what small-town life was like, and would be willing to endure it again. He wrote that if I intended to accept, I needed to send in my transcripts and complete the necessary paperwork within the month. I thought carefully about it and decided I wanted to do this. I just didn't know if Terrence would be willing to move there with me. I needed to talk to him, but those talks turned out to be difficult.

"And what exactly would I do, Toby? I suspect there are no restaurants or bars there where I could get a job. Could I get a janitorial job there? Would you want to live with me? And where would we live? Would I still be your 'Chicago cousin'? Small towns are notorious for being unaccepting. What kind of life would we have?"

The questions went on. I could not answer any of them. We talked and argued. He continued to review reasons the two of us could not live in Everstille. I knew he was correct. Then he explained how, in a big city like Chicago, even with the strictures and limitations of society we could make a life for ourselves. I agreed. He suggested that we each find another part-time job and save money. In just a few years, because the economy was slowly improving, we might be able to find a small row-house to purchase. I didn't answer. Even Terrence knew he was stretching the facts. We finally stopped discussing the issue.

As the time grew closer for a decision, I realized that I didn't want to leave Terrence, but needed to consider the future. He was upset, and I was too, but living in the tiny apartment, working part-time jobs, and not using the skills I knew I had developed in college and through substitute teaching was a waste. And if I were to be honest with myself, I was not happy living this double life. We went a few days without talking, and I made up my mind. I took the job. I sent in my papers along with an inquiry about a place to live, and Clarence Jenkins answered with suggestions and ideas and a couple names to contact. Terry and I began to speak again, but this time, it was not about my staying in Chicago.

Summer was ending. I had not been hired to do much substitute teaching during the summer school session and had plenty of time to visit my family who were sad to see me go but glad I had obtained a teaching position. Mother was even excited that I was going back to Everstille, and she hinted that she would come and visit and maybe see some old friends there. I told her I would come back to Chicago to visit her and my sisters and their families. However, she came to Everstille only once, and that was when Ruth and I married. I did visit her a few times a year because I came back to Chicago, but the visits were to see Terry. Mother and he were never introduced. It was better that way.

Late in the summer, a couple weeks before the school session was to begin, I packed my belongings: clothes, personal effects, books, odds and ends. I put everything in my car upon which I had spent some of my diminishing money to ensure it would run smoothly, and prepared to set off. It was a very early Monday morning. Terry and I had said our good-byes the previous day, and he was still sleeping. I moved quietly around the small rooms getting ready to leave, placing the remainder of my belongings in a bag. I took a last look around at the place I had lived with Terry. I glanced at the closed bedroom door behind which he was sleeping, then softly opened the apartment door and left. The apartment key was on the kitchen table next to a gift for him. He had admired an imported black and white silk tie which I bought for him leaving it alongside a brief note containing my new address. I departed then because I was afraid Terry would attempt once again to talk me into staying. I was afraid that I would.

I walked out of the building and crossed the street to where my parked and packed car was waiting. I checked everything out once more and put my hand on the door to open it. I should not have turned to look up at our apartment window, but I did. Terry was standing there watching me. I think he had pretended to sleep because he had not wanted to risk another good-by any more than I had. We stood for a few seconds looking at each other. Then I threw the bag I was clutching onto the passenger seat, got into the car, started it, and drove off.

Good-byes are a sad business, Livie, a sad business.

6. September 30

I was so busy the first month of that first year that I was unable to write to Terry until the end of September. I wrote consistently to him every week after that, but received few replies. When I did, it was a brief note, lacking in details, and hardly worth the postage stamp. But we kept up a correspondence of sorts, and on a weekend in October, I took the first of what would turn out to be many trips back to Chicago to be with him. I would leave right after school on Friday and return Sunday night. About every other third or fourth time I visited Terry, I drove to see my family on Sunday afternoon before returning. I always explained to them I had been in the area for a meeting or seminar or some such thing. I admit to not being honest but felt I needed to protect everyone, especially my mother, from the truth.

Teaching at Everstille High School was enjoyable. The students were easier to manage than I expected, and I appreciated the experiences I had in Chicago schools which taught me how to handle difficult situations. Because I was on the swim team when I was younger, I was asked to start one. There was a newly built pool in the school and it wanted use. Between the team practices and teaching duties, I had little time to create new friendships, so when Ruth Evans and I became friends, it was both surprising and appreciated.

As strange as it may seem to you, Livie, your Aunt Anne was one of my first students. She was miles ahead of the other students in her class when it came to reading, interpreting, and writing about literature, and that was all due, as I found out later, to your mother's teaching and training of her. When I wanted to introduce my students to a writing project that needed researching, I went to the public library in town, where I discovered that Anne, who worked there, and your mother, the Head Librarian, had amassed some of the best research material I had seen. Titles were up-to-date, the research process had been stream-lined by Ruth, and both she and Anne were experts in finding information. I was excited to begin this project, and Ruth was a tremendous help. We worked together, planning and organizing, and while the first papers were a disappointment, Ruth encouraged me to assign another. By the third assignment, students were beginning to catch on, something all teachers are happy for, and Ruth and I had created a solid friendship.

I have mentioned before that I was not particularly comfortable with women, but Ruth changed that. I have often ruminated on our friendship, trying to parse out exactly what it was that brought us together, and I have decided that it was all due to Ruth. She was extremely intelligent. She was curious and inventive and patient. She was a deep reader who meticulously dissected what she read and supported her opinions fastidiously with concrete examples from the text. We enjoyed discussing both the newest literature and the classics, and, while I don't believe in fate or karma, I marvel at the providence that brought us together. If you have half her intelligence, you will still be smarter that most of the people you will meet in your life.

My teaching/coaching duties, the bourgeoning friendship with Ruth, and periodic travels to see Terry kept me busy. Time passed and I was happy in Everstille as an adult in a way I never had been as a child. Ruth and I ended up going to various civic activities together, and I was invited to her house where she and her uncle, Doctor Evans, and I engaged in enjoyable Sunday afternoon discussions on their back porch. At least on those Sundays I was not with Terrence.

Ruth trusted me, and I believed she could keep my secrets, and after a couple years, when our friendship seemed proved, I shared with her my greatest secret. I told her about Terrence Douglas. I explained where I was on those weekends I would leave Everstille and travel to Chicago. She was accepting and understanding and conscientiously promised me she would say nothing. The only time anyone else was told was when Anne was taken into our confidence. That was after Terry moved in with us. After your mother and I married.

I was a few years into teaching when the principal, Clarence Jenkins, called me into his office one day after classes and closed the door. He asked me to sit down, and he sat back at his desk and leaned against his old swivel chair.

"Toby, I am going to retire at the end of this year. I am getting older, and it's time for a younger man to take over the business of being principal. There was a short-list generated by the school board to consider some teachers for the job, and you were on that list. It was narrowed down to two names, and yours was one. Soon the board will come to me, and I'll pretend to think about it for a while, but I will be telling them that you are my choice for the job. Are you willing to take it?'

I sat still for a while and thought before I spoke. "Principal Jenkins, I am honored that you are so supportive of me, and I am willing and excited to take the job, but are you sure I'm the right person?" I was astounded at his being so blunt with me.

"I have the right person. The other man on the list is Jim

Reynolds, and frankly, the man gets on my nerves. That, of course, is between us as is this entire conversation."

"Yes, Sir, I understand."

"Jim is an acceptably mediocre teacher and an adequate coach, but he would be a miserable principal. I have put my life into this school and hate to see it destroyed by someone who finds it difficult to keep his classroom organized and the football team uniforms from getting lost. I wanted to talk to you before the next school board meeting and let you know that you should get your resume and transcripts ready for it. I believe Mrs. Green has an official letter for you when you leave here. I know Jim Reynolds has been given his. Anyway, get your ducks in a row and get ready. Any questions?"

I had a few, but thought they could wait until I went home to think about them. I thanked Principal Jenkins, and we stood as he walked me to his closed door. He held out his hand and we shook.

"One more thing, Toby. The only advantage Jim Reynolds has over you is that he is married. I know that the board would, for some reason, Lord knows why, like to have the principal a married man. Jim's wife, Marianne, has been able to push out five kids in their ten years together, and you can't get more married then that. While it's not a requirement, the school board has this as their prejudice, so I want to give you a head's up. Don't know your romantic life, and don't want to, but the town's rumor mill has had you and Ruth Evans married for a while now. Just give some thought to your future. And hers."

We shook hands again and as I left. Mrs. Green handed me an official letter, whispered, "Good luck!" and smiled.

I went home to read the letter and sat down to think. It was a Wednesday evening, and I was meeting Ruth at Mazie's for the blue-plate special and a discussion of our latest reading. I knew I could not tell her anything yet, but when the time came, she would be the first person I told. And soon that time came. Your mother and I had many discussions after that, Livie, and not all of them were amiable.

I hear you crying. You are getting more teeth and are bothered by them, so I will stop here for tonight and check on you and attempt to soothe you. Perhaps we will rock in the rocking chair Terry bought for your room; the one in which your mother meant to rock you. I'll rock you tonight. Perhaps that will comfort both of us.

7. October 13

Despite my bachelor status, I was offered the position of Everstille High School principal, a job I still hold. Clarence Jenkins remained for a few months over the summer session and into the fall semester, to steer me and make sure, as he said, I "had my footing". He was an excellent mentor, and since his death, I miss our discussions and his guidance. Clarence directed me through the meetings and reports and general paperwork the position required, and while that was useful, the process was more humdrum than difficult, and I caught on quickly. I owe Principal Jenkins much for assisting me through the difficulties that occurred that first year, especially through the problems generated by Jim Reynolds.

Rumors in a school spread quickly, and soon the information that I would be the new principal was known. I was in the teachers' lunchroom with Mrs. Waxton, head of the English Department, and a couple other teachers when Jim Reynolds came in. He strode over to me as I was taking a seat, grabbed my hand and shook it. Hard. Jim is shorter than me, but big and burly with a stomach that was, to be kind, rotund. He spoke much louder than necessary as he congratulated me and promised that there were no hard feelings because he did not get the position. He smiled at Mrs. Waxton, reshook my hand, and strode out of the room. There was complete silence for a few seconds. Then Mrs. Waxton leaned forward to quote, "'O! beware, my lord, of jealousy. It is the green-eyed monster…'" I was going to ask her to expound on the comment as she was clearly referring to Jim Reynolds, but a few more teachers came into the room, and I did not want to start that discussion. She just raised her eyebrows and began to eat her ham sandwich as general talking filled the air. If you are not familiar with Shakespeare, Livie, I suspect you will be after reading this.

I decided I would not worry about Mrs. Waxton's comment but instead, concentrate on my job. Summer break came, and Principal Jenkins and I spent the weeks overseeing the summer term and organizing the next school year. Fall came, and I will admit, the first month was a difficult one. I spent each passing period in the halls greeting students, moving them along to their classes, establishing myself as the main authority figure in the school, as per Principal Jenkins' counsel. After a few weeks, it seemed to me that things were going smoothly. Then the first incident happened.

It was a Monday morning during passing time between first

and second period, and I was on the second-floor stairwell greeting and encouraging everyone to move quickly to the next class. Suddenly, from behind, I was pushed, and then almost immediately, an arm reached out to grab me and kept me from falling down the stairs. I don't think the push was an accident because I felt a hand on my back and a definite push outwards. I lost my footing and grabbed the bannister but was grateful for the unknown arm which saved me. Once I regained my balance, I swirled around as a crowd of boys rushed down the stairs. I waited until the hallways cleared and then walked back to the office where I decided it was just an accident. Then on Wednesday, something similar happened.

This time, I was near the Gymnasium doors. I was not standing very close to them as I was aware which way they would open, but towards the end of the passing time, a group pushed out flinging the door open much wider than necessary, and one door hit my shoulder so hard that later it bruised. I turned to see who the boys were, and one of them yelled out, "Oops, sorry Principal P., didn't see you," although two large windows in the gym doors allowed for viewing. I scrutinized the boys to try and figure out which one could have yelled the apology, but the crowd rushed by, and as they did, there was a burst of laughter from them. It was possible someone said something funny, but a couple of them glanced over their shoulders at me. As I looked at them, two things occurred to me. First, this seemed to be the same bunch that passed me on the staircase Monday, and secondly, most of the students appeared to be members of the football team.

I waited for another incident to happen, but nothing did that week. The following Monday, our janitor, Mr. Spellers came to see me.

"Um, Mr. Pinkerton, the students at this school are pretty good kids, but recently I've had to clean off some stuff written in the boys' bathroom on the first floor and in the boys' gym locker room. I wiped it clean twice last week, but I just checked, and it's there again. I think you should see it."

We went to the bathroom first and then the locker room. Now, generally, teachers have thick skins. If they don't, they won't last long. So, when I saw what was written about me on those walls, my feelings weren't hurt, but I was aggravated about the school property being defaced and creating additional work for Mr. Spellers. I thanked him for bringing it to my attention and asked him to clean it off and let me know if it appeared again. Then I went back to the office to consider the situation. I sat down at my desk and after some thought, called Clarence Jenkins. We spoke at length.

What was written was unimportant, and I'm not sure I even remember the wording. What bothered me was the grain of knowledge in it. The comments were references to my private life and what I did in my spare time. And it was not about swimming or reading. I thought back to Mrs. Waxton's comment and the group of boys I was sure I had identified.

That day after school, when football practice was being held, I went to the field behind the school and stood and watched. I made sure Jim Reynolds saw me, then stood for the better part of thirty minutes before I waved to Jim and left. I also went on Wednesday, and when the team won their game on Friday afternoon, I made sure to congratulate them as them came into the locker room where I was standing, waiting for them. Then I left to find Jim Reynolds and congratulate him. I wasn't sure if I had pinpointed the correct group and their mentor, but I thought I had. I began to think about what Clarence Jenkins said about marriage, and about Mrs. Waxton's comment, and reviewed the incidents over the three weeks. It was fitting together, and I needed to make some decisions.

It took a couple more months of vigilant, careful watching on my part to conclude that the covert jealousy Jim Reynolds felt about my becoming principal manifested in what I assumed was a sly, subtle encouragement of the type of incidents that occasionally happened. There weren't many. I was pushed once more during a fire drill, but that may have been accidental. There were a few more wall writings, and a message went out to the student body about the penalties connected with school vandalism. At the same time, I continued intermittent visits to football practices. And I found ways to deal with Jim Reynolds. I knew he had a large family, and his salary just barely met their needs. There were various meetings I asked Jim to chair, and a small stipend was attached to these duties. And, now, Livie, you might consider that this was a form of bribery. You would be correct.

While one problem seemed to be solved, I suspected it was only temporary. A long-term solution was needed. For the first time, I was thinking seriously about marriage. I have nothing against the institution. I understand its societal, religious, and economic purposes. My parents' marriage was a happy one, and both my sisters seem to be satisfied with their husbands and families. But, given my nature and perspective, I never seriously thought marriage was for me. And here I was, considering it. And considering it with the only woman I could ever marry: my best friend, Ruth Evans.

Ruth knew all about the school incidents, my suspicion about

Jim Reynolds, and everything else connected with my principal job. She knew it all because I told her everything. Except for one thing. I never mentioned the marriage advice Principal Jenkins gave me. That subject was touchy. We had discussed the fact that marriage was not in our individual futures. Certainly not in our collective future either. Ruth told me about her parents' expectation for her to marry their farmer neighbor, and the arguments she and her father had. She knew about Terrence and why I would not marry. And then, I brought the topic of marriage, our marriage, up to her and did so more than once.

The first time, she laughed. The second time, she seemed angry. And by the third time I talked about the two of us marrying, she realized I was serious.

"Ruth, we are best friends. There are so many reasons for a marriage between us, and not just to save my job and stop nasty rumors. I respect you enough to admit this is part of the reason, but think about it. Think about us growing older by ourselves. We could be together. We enjoy the same things and go together to most of the same meetings and events. Finances would be easier for both of us. Of course, we would need to discuss certain things, but I know we could work it out."

I talked and explained, and Ruth listened. Periodically she would comment or ask something, but we never came to an agreement. This went on for months. We went together to the annual church potluck, the high school drama club play, the civic organizations' Christmas parties, and when Anne's family had a New Year's Eve get-together, we were invited. Then something happened and the new year brought changes.

Ruth lived with her uncle, Doctor Evans. She had moved in with him when she took the job at the library and had never moved out. They were both content with the situation and saw no reason to change. But Doctor Evans was retiring and had decided to relocate down South where his youngest sister lived and had asked him to move in with her. Because Ruth could not afford to purchase the large Victorian house on her own, it was going to be sold. At the same time, Anne's parents sold their farm, were looking to move into town, and Anne was looking for a place to live on her own because she thought it was time for her to live a life separate from her parents. Knowing all this, I used this time to bring up marriage to Ruth again and suggest that between us, if we married, we could buy the house that she loved. Anne could take over my apartment lease, and this appeared to be a perfect solution to a series of problems. This time, Ruth promised to think about it seriously.

Well, Livie, I don't need to explain the obvious. Your mother and I married. Our wedding was a small affair which took place over Spring Break. We bought and then moved into this large Victorian house, Anne moved into my apartment on Charming Lane, and Doctor Evans retired to live with his sister. I remember that week in part because it was the first time Ruth and I argued. Ever. And the argument was about Terry.

It's late and I am tired. I need to figure out exactly what I want to write next. I wish I could simply sit down nightly and get this story told, but sometimes I just need to break between writing sessions, and this is one of those times. It is beginning to be fall and the weather vacillates between cool and humid, and tonight is one of those humid nights. Terry is out on the back porch, and I think I will go and talk to him for a while. Till next time.

8. October 20

During that first year as principal, Ruth and I often discussed the possibility of marrying. At the same time, I continued to take trips to Chicago so that Terry and I could be together. The assumption by Everstille citizenry was that I was visiting my family, which I sometimes did, or I was taking a class or was busy at seminars and lectures. There was no need to challenge these beliefs. In summer, I was able to get away for at least two weeks, and once, I stayed almost a month. Ruth knew where I was and how to get in touch with me in case of an emergency. Terry continued working at the restaurant in Chicago, but was always glad to see me, and I was glad to see him, spend time in the small apartment, and visit with other friends I missed.

Terry knew about Ruth just as she knew about him. I kept no secrets from either of them, and Terry understood why we married. When Ruth and I married and got settled and organized, I took a weekend to visit him. He had a girlfriend, Betsy, at the time, and he spoke to me about possibly marrying her. That did not happen. Terry was not a marrying man either. Ironic for me to write that having married your mother.

Before we married, Ruth and I talked at length about my relationship with Terry. She knew our marriage would not be a typical one and understood I planned to continue my visits to Chicago. I don't think she expected me to visit with the regularity I did, and that was the cause of our arguments. It doesn't matter what we said; neither of us wanted or intended to hurt the other.

I thought I could solve the problem. In hindsight, I was selfish and looked for a solution that would solve my own misery. Misery in being away from Terry and misery at making Ruth unhappy. *The miserable have no other medicine, but only hope,* claimed Shakespeare, and I hoped my plan would work. When I proposed to Ruth that Terry move in with us, there were additional disagreements and discussions. Eventually, she said she would be willing to have him move in for what she called a "trial basis". Other stipulations were made, and I was quick to concede. Once Ruth agreed, I spent a considerable amount of time talking to Terry about the move. I had to convince him to leave his Chicago home and job and friends for an uncertain future in Everstille. When he agreed to the trial basis, I was delighted. I was also nervous about the outcome. I hoped both Terry and Ruth would like each other and get along, and I was unsure either would happen.

For a few months after Terry moved in with us, the two of them circled each other like cats, and I was concerned. We all knew that our situation was unusual, at best. But I had faith in them and was sure the three of us could live together and be content. It took some time, but eventually they got used to each other, came to like each other, and then…well that is still to be explained.

I think here I need to clarify our living arrangements since you are old enough to wonder about them. When your mother and I moved into this house, she took the large master bedroom on the first floor for hers. There was a smaller room next to it that we used as an office, and, once you were expected, it became your nursery. I made one of the three bedrooms upstairs mine. When Terry moved in, he took the third bedroom upstairs, the one farthest back, as his. Since your birth, I have moved downstairs to be close to you. This situation, perhaps strange, suited all of us. *There is nothing good or bad, but thinking makes it so*, and sorry, Livie, more Shakespeare.

Livie, there are so many things I can't bring myself to write about. I have stumbled over this section, writing, and rewriting and tearing it up again and again. I can only be pressed so far. There are memories which are hurtful and others which are sweet, and sometimes they overlap. I can't stress enough that whatever difficulties there have been, however many times I have blamed myself for things that happened, I would do it all again knowing that your young, loving and accepting presence would become the center of this household.

It is not very late, but I will stop here. I know I must write about Terrence and your mother, but can't manage that just now. He is downstairs tonight, so I will end this now and think about what I should tell you. Perhaps I will discuss it with him.

Sweet dreams, Livie.

9. October 25

I am going to deviate a bit tonight and write about you. The fall weather is wonderful, and this last Sunday, just as she usually is on that day, Anne was here. We raked leaves and showed you how to jump into a pile of them. You laughed and played, and when the weather became windy and cold, and it appeared that rain was going to fall, you asserted what Terry calls your "independence" and ran away from all of us, making us chase you until eventually Anne caught you. We hurriedly put the rakes and brooms away and got inside to warm up.

Once inside, Terry built a fire, and Anne made hot chocolate which she served with her home-made cookies. The four of us were comfortable and warm before the fireplace as the weather took a turn and a torrential rain began. You cuddled against Anne as she read the Golden Books to you that you love, and eventually you dozed off as she cradled you. I tell you this because I know you won't remember it. I want you to know that your childhood is as happy and normal as the three of us can make it even though Ruth is gone. Nothing would or could take the place of your mother, and while you slept, the three of us reminisced about her.

You have your mother's intelligence. We have pictures of her around the house, and both Terry and I point them out to you daily. You have taken to pointing from your crib to the rocking chair and saying "Mama, Mama", but I think you are simply pointing at the picture which is on a nearby table. I am teaching you some simple bedtime prayers, and we always end "I send my love to Mama in Heaven." Of course, you don't understand this tradition yet, but one day you will. Terrence and Anne and I discuss what traditions we will help create for you, and we have decided upon some.

You enjoy learning about colors, and for a few months you wanted all things a bright banana yellow. This is probably due to the soft yellow toy banana someone gave you. When Terry decided to repaint your nursery this bright color, you loved watching him move the brush and change the walls from green to yellow. I needed to hold you while he painted so that you would not run into the still wet walls. Once the room was dry and we replaced things, you crawled up to the wall to touch it, and for a long time, you would touch the yellow and then turn and laugh. Lately, you seem to gravitate towards pink. Terry thought it would be fun to repaint your room each year with your new favorite color. We decided that for your birthday, we would do that. Terry has unusual ideas about raising a child. I think it was because his childhood was so dreary and dismal. Anyway, next birthday, if you are still leaning towards pink, that is what the birthday color will be.

We also thought that you should be able to choose the kind of cake and the special dinner for your birthday. This may not happen for a few years, but eventually you will have specific tastes. These ideas are simple and our way of giving you choices in life. I wonder how many coats of paint walls can take? I suspect that eventually, you may want to move from the nursery to another bedroom, so the walls in the nursery may have a break after a few years.

We have already started the tradition of Anne coming over on Sundays and being responsible for your nighttime bath and bedtime story. She is currently enamored of all the Golden Books which are available, and whenever she finds a new one at the Emporium in town, she purchases it and brings it over to add to your growing collection. Books, as Anne tells us, will absolutely be a large part of your life as they are to her, and were to your mother.

We are going to spend holidays here, in our home. We know invitations will come from many kind and generous people, but Terry and I agree that we should make the holidays a special time for you in our house. We want Anne to be here too. She said she will need to spend time with her family which is understandable, but because she is so much a part of your life, we would like her here as often as possible. I sometimes feel guilty about taking Anne away from what should be a life of her own, and Terry and I have talked about it with her. She said that we, together, make up your family, and that is the way she wants it to be. The three of us are so comfortable together that we really do feel like a family. I believe part of this is because Ruth knew she could trust Anne with our secrets, and she was correct. We can trust her and have even asked her to consider moving into this house. However, she said that will not happen. She says the town has had enough to gossip about and anyway, she could never take Ruth's place. She is, as I have said before, aggravatingly right about most things.

Halloween is coming up in a few days, and while you don't really understand it yet, the adults are looking forward to it. Anne found a costume for you. We decided not to show it to you yet because we think you will want to wear it all the time. It is a tiger costume and has a long tail, and we are sure you are going to be fascinated with it because you love to drag your stuffed animals by their tails and hold them up and say "tal, tal". Your attempts to talk are both amusing and astounding.

I know I have not exactly stuck to the thesis of this lengthy letter, but I wanted you to know Terrence and Anne and I look forward to every weekday and weekend and holiday with you. We will happily paint your room a new birthday color yearly, and I suspect you will soon have every Golden Book Anne can find. You are only missing one thing, and there is nothing we can do about that.

I hear Terry who has finished up with your bath and is reading you a book. I am looking forward to going to your bedroom and saying your bedtime prayer with you and hearing you say "I send my love to Mama in Heaven". Then I will kiss your beautiful red hair and watch as you close your eyes. Perhaps I will sleep tonight too.

10. November 26

This next part is difficult, and I have put off writing it for long enough. Terry told me to write whatever I think I should, and that is the problem. This next part, this part about your mother and Terrence is not mine to write. I can only explain my feelings about the situation, and for this reason, cannot write details. However, I believe I have convinced him to tell his story in writing. I have given him this document to read and told him to change anything he wants. He said there is nothing to change but complained about my comparison of Ruth and him to cats circling each other. He said he would prefer being compared to dogs, and that made me laugh. Finally, Terry said he will consider writing down his story although it will not be as lengthy as this. I told him the length was unimportant. Only the content matters. I also told him that I did not want to read what he wrote. It is his story to tell you, and only the two of you should know it. I will adhere to that.

Your mother told me she was expecting a child. She was expecting you. That is how I will begin. My first emotions were anger and shock and surprise. Then I was hurt and felt betrayed, and then, as issues became evident, as I began to consider realities. I accepted, then settled, then welcomed this newness. That is the evolution. It did not happen overnight but took months, and there were instances when I reverted to an earlier emotion. But the result was that the three of us: your mother, Terrence, and I, formed a unit. A family unit. And as peculiar as that seems, it happened.

At first, the feelings were sickeningly overwhelming. I had difficulty concentrating on my job, and I know it was noticed. Mrs. Green, my school secretary, in her kind, motherly fashion, inquired whether everything was satisfactory, and then began to feed me her home-baked goods. I admit that my appetite was lost for a while, and I could not eat. On my tall frame, it showed.

There was a quiet and tension in our house that was new. I found plenty to keep me busy at school and stayed late most days. I began to appear at all the school sports practices and to attend various club meetings. Anything to stay away from the house. Ruth, too, worked late. The library was undergoing its renovation and expansion, and that was her excuse. Terry began to leave earlier for work than necessary. He came home at his usual time, but the house remained empty until later, and to fill up the time, he threw himself into painting and repairing things which were already in good shape. During this month or so we all stayed apart,

I suspect we were all doing the same thing…considering where this journey would take us.

Eventually, we reunited. One evening, Ruth and I arrived home at the same time and walked into the house where a delicious aroma met us. Terry was in the kitchen cooking, and we went to see what he was making. Ruth began to set the table, and I started to ask Terrence about his day, and all of us sat down to eat a dinner together. Something which we had not been doing. We talked that night and started to heal. It took time, but we came to terms about what had happened, and our relationships, and we agreed there was a new purpose for us. That purpose was you.

Ruth had been doing research into pregnancies and babies and had determined she would give birth at home. About half the women in Everstille continued to have home births, and because neither Terrence nor I had any first-hand experience with this, we thought it would work. I wish now that we had not so readily agreed. But Ruth was adamant about this and explained her reasons to us and to Doctor Grenville in her usual carefully researched and thorough manner. She had additional ideas about where she would deliver you. Towards the back area in the kitchen is a large, unused room which was once the housekeeper's quarters. Ruth wanted this room to be the "birthing room" and had plans for its cleaning and redecorating. The smaller room next to her bedroom would be changed into a nursery. So, over the months before your birth, the three of us worked on these projects.

We were content during this time. Terry and I did most of the heavy labor, and Ruth, growing larger and larger, would instruct us and explain what she wanted done. We followed her directions and took her advice. She had specific ideas about the nursery color and the furniture placement, and through the cleaning and painting and readying the house for you, the three of us grew closer. We fell into our previous pattern of laughing and joking with each other, and we discussed forthrightly and honestly the situation in which we found ourselves. We realized our circumstance was peculiar, and outsiders would not understand or condone it, so we agreed to kept it to ourselves. We also made decisions about you and how the three of us, with Anne's help, would approach your upbringing, what you would be taught to call us, and how we would handle issues which were sure to arise. Honestly, we found ourselves in a perplexing arrangement, and I am unsure I completely understand it still. Terry had been introduced to everyone in Everstille as my "Chicago cousin" and was accepted as such. Ruth and I were married, and she was your mother. I was, legally, your father. Those were our roles.

After the holidays and into the early spring, when Ruth's condition could not be hidden, she had to resign from her job at the library. Anne was her very strong recommendation as her replacement, and the Library Board agreed. I know that her time spent at home and not at the library was difficult for your mother. She had worked many years as Head Librarian, and the townspeople came to admire and depend on her. She encouraged reading groups to meet and children to gather for what she called "Read-Aloud Stories". Ruth was exceptional at fund-raising, and I don't think she was ever turned down when she solicited additional monies from various civic organizations and private parties for library purchases, and she significantly increased the library's holdings. She also artfully supported female authors by advertising their books in her "Authors You Should Know" corner and kept an up-to-date collection of women authors' books. Ruth was utterly influential, calmly forceful, and quietly amazing. My heart breaks to know that you will never have her extraordinary guidance.

I informed my sisters that Ruth was expecting in a few months, and she also wrote to the one sister with whom she still corresponded, and they sent gifts for you and indifferent congratulations for us. Neither Ruth nor I kept up timely communication with our families. Terrence had no family, and the three of us agreed that our living situation would probably not be understood by them. We, along with Anne, made up our own family. As far as we could tell, the town had accepted Terrence as a permanent member of the household because he was my relative. There was a tale, an explanation, that both Terry and I had to tell others after your birth, and I will enlighten you about it further on in this missive.

So, Livie, for some months, before you were born, Ruth and Terry, and I lived together and were content. We had discussed our situation, sometimes rather loudly, but at the end, we were determined to create a loving and nurturing home for you. One in which you would grow up happy, gratified, and cherished, and that is still our intention.

Ruth accepted that she would be at home to raise you, but she always intended to return to the library in some capacity, and she and Anne often discussed the future and what it would look like. We readied the birthing room and the nursery for you. Ruth was given a baby shower by the women of our church, and all of us enjoyed looking over the gifts you received. Anne was excited to deliver the buggy which you currently still use, and there were times we just smiled and laughed at what we were positive would be a joyous and contented future for all of us.

O God, that one might read the book of fate, and see the revolution of the times wrote the Bard. Although I am not sure either Terrence or I would have wanted to see what the future held for us all. We were all content in our happiness then, and by your presence, you have gladdened our lives again.

11. November 28

Your mother was tall but slender, and until the last three months or so of carrying you, did not appear to be expecting. She was violently ill for the first couple months as her body adjusted to this change, but after that, until the last month or so, Ruth seemed healthy and strong. She was forty when you were born, and apparently that was not in her favor. I have spent many hours in conversation with Doctor Grenville discussing what exactly happened. He did not have a clear answer, and without becoming too graphic and upsetting, Terrence and I decided that when she died, we would not allow her poor body to undergo any more trauma, even though Doctor Grenville encouraged us to find out exactly what happened. Terms like *postpartum infection* and *phlebitis* and *puerperal fever* were discussed, and finally, I stopped talking to the doctor about the *Why?* As I write this, I pray that you are not too upset about these words. Do not squander your emotions with guilt created by my writing the truth to you. Ruth loved you. And her last day on earth was spent holding and talking to you during her times of consciousness.

Your mother died on an early Monday morning. We were advised to leave you at the hospital for a week or so until we got through the funeral, but neither Terry nor I could bear to think you were alone with no one to visit, so, we hired a nurse to care for you and brought you home Tuesday night. Neither one of us slept much the first few weeks. We took turns sitting with you in the rocking chair Terry bought for your mother. He rocked you, and I tried to sleep, and then we switched. There was probably no need to do that. You were, and are, a calm, contented child, not very crabby or particularly fussy, but holding you was a form of grieving for your mother in a way that was both sorrowful and comforting.

I don't think either of us were prepared for the show of love Everstille had for Ruth, and we were stunned by the books offered up to her at the funeral. They were donations; they were presents; they were thanks. Anne has almost completed organizing, cataloging, and preparing the *Ruth Books*, as they are called, for the new library room which has been dedicated to your mother. By this time, I know you will be familiar with the *Ruth Evans Pinkerton Room* at the library and aware of the story of the many books there. Anne will see to that. She is already reading books to you and for your birthday, gifted you additional new Golden Books. *Ten Little Fingers*, *So This is Spring*, and *Raggedy Ann's Tea Party* are currently your favorites, and the Raggedy Ann doll she brought to accompany that book goes to bed nightly with you. Tonight, both Terry and I were required to bestow multiple kisses on both your face and little Raggedy Ann's painted one before you could sleep. You delight us.

We spent last Thanksgiving with Anne's family because we were simply too exhausted to plan much and took advantage of a kind offer. But when we came home and put you to bed, Terrence and I discussed our own family traditions. It is important that we not rely on others, but fashion our own rituals and practices so that you grow up with a sense of them. Anne, as often as she is able, will be included in these celebrations. We will not be going out this Thanksgiving but will be spending it at home, hopefully with Anne, making a dinner and enjoying it together.

Last Christmas, you were still too young, and will not remember this, but we took a trip to South Bend for a special day during which we ate a wonderful lunch at one of the new restaurants there and afterwards, went to Robertson's Department Store to choose a special Christmas tree ornament. Terry held up two different ones, and the one you tried to grab first was the one we bought. This year you will be older and should be able to make your own choice. Our first Christmas tree was a small one, but Anne was here to help decorate it, and we clapped when she held you and helped to place your ornament on the tree. Terry snapped a picture with his camera to mark the occasion. Another tradition.

There was much discussion about what to do for your birthday. There is both glee and sadness connected with that time, so we have decided to simply celebrate it as your day. There will be a small party and as you grow older and have specific tastes, you will be able to choose what we have for your birthday dinner and the type of cake you want. It will be a cheerful time. Ruth's passing will have its own observation a couple weeks later, so as not to spoil the gladness of your day.

There are flowers planted in Ruth's garden plot behind the house, and this year, one Saturday, a few weeks after your first birthday, we went to visit your mother's grave. Ruth loved to bake, and her cinnamon cake was always special. Terry used her recipe and baked one for us to take with us and share when we visited North Cemetery. Before leaving, we took you to the flower garden and helped you gather some of the early blooms. There were some late lilacs left, and we cut some branches to place on her grave. We decided that for this tradition, it would just be the three of us remembering your mother. Anne is welcomed, but she has her own tradition for honoring Ruth, her mentor and best friend.

Tonight, after we left, you snuggled up to Raggedy Ann, Terry went to his room, and I came here to the desk to continue my writing. I have just returned to it because I could hear you in your room chattering, and I went to check on you. As I came in, you were sitting up and having a conversation with, I assume yourself, or your doll. I peeked around the corner and when you saw me, you pointed to the area where a small table is placed next to the rocking chair and said, "Mama". We keep several pictures of Ruth around the house. Terry has one in his room, I have another in mine, and we placed one on the table in your room. You kiss it good-night. Watching you point and chatter made me feel that you do understand who Ruth is, and that makes me glad. Oh, if she were only here to watch over you and teach you. She was a wonderful and accepting person, Livie, and although I am not the marrying type, I am gladdened when I think that I did marry my best friend, your mother, Ruth Evans.

12. December 6

I am coming to the end of my script, Livie. I want you to know that should you have more questions, and want answers, I will give them to you. I promise to be truthful and hope you feel there is freedom in coming to me. Or to Terrence. We are just starting our journey together, the three of us, and will need to work at finding our way.

There is something I alluded to a couple of entries back, something about a tale Terry and I told after you were born. During last summer, when the weather was kind and neither too hot or humid, the two of us pushed your buggy down Main Street, and walked along, stopping at the Emporium and the bakery, and buying a few needed items. It was busy, being Saturday, and many of Everstille's citizens stopped to both express their continued condolences about Ruth and to admire you and see your features. There is no denying your hair color. It is the same as Terrence's. We explained to those who commented on it, and that was everyone, that Terrence's family had the copper /red hair and since we are cousins, we share some of the same traits which showed up in you. Because I am a teacher, and now, a principal, my pseudo-scientific explanation seemed to be accepted. I explain this because I believe you may be questioned as you grow up, and this is what I will tell you. And this is what you will be told to say to those who may question your parentage.

I don't expect life without a mother will be easy for you, Livie. Anne will be here and available for those instances when a woman is necessary. I am grateful for her help. So is Terry. She is one of the very few people who know the truth for sure. Ruth was so sure of Anne's understanding and acceptance that she insisted you be named after her. We were happy to name you Olivia Anne.

Terry says he will write his story soon. He intends to do it all at one time to get it done, and plans to spend part of his vacation time doing it. When completed, he'll give it to Anne for safekeeping, the same as I will give this to her tomorrow. We discussed what your future will look like and how you will feel once these missives have been given to you. Anne said she will keep them safe until you are an adult and will be able to process this story…your story. We all agreed that should you ask questions before you are old enough to read this, we will answer them honestly. Of course, your age will determine what we say, how we approach the truth.

Life is inexplicable and puzzling. We are all strange creatures,

Livie, and, as Shakespeare wrote:

> *All the world's a stage, And all the men and women merely*
> *players;*
> *They have their exits and their entrances;*
> *And one man in his life plays many parts.*

The part I play now is your mother's widowed husband, whose last name you share, and whom you call,

Dada

Tobias Pinkerton

Terrence Douglas

Written the week after Christmas, 1955

Dear Little Cabbage,

I have some time off, and it is cold, and Christmas is over. I am starting this in the afternoon as you are napping, and Toby said he will take care of you while I get this completed. I want to continue writing until I am done otherwise, I am afraid I won't succeed. So, here goes.

I have been forced into writing to you. That's a bad choice of words. Of course, I want you to know about your family and background, but I read what Toby wrote, and it seems like it's all there. I want to do what's best for you, but I guess Toby and Anne are right. They think I might be able to add something to our story. I suppose there are some things I can tell you. Maybe, because you are reading this and are much older, you already know them. Perhaps I have told you things. But in case I haven't, I'll try to do it now. This letter will be short. I can't write as good as Toby can and don't have the patience he does.

I grew up in Chicago with my mother and younger brother, Thomas. In fact, if you had been a boy, we were going to name you after him. Didn't turn out that way. Tommy and me and Mom lived in a small apartment in a neighborhood on Chicago's south side and things were rough growing up. Tommy was born when I was four, and then my father left. Mom never much spoke about him or about that time, and I have no idea where he went or why he left, or what happened to him. I don't have a picture of him, but I do remember he had red hair like mine. And Tommy's. And yours. That's the saddest part of my life. Until your mother died. When Tommy was about four (and I was eight), there was a bad influenza going around, and Tommy got it and died. Mom was working as a seamstress in a factory and she got sick too, but she lived. At least long enough to bury Tom and find me a place where I could live and be safe, and then she died too.

There was a family who lived on the next street and the woman and Mom were friends. They had worked together, and I guess Mom did a great favor for the woman, Jenny. I never knew what the favor was, but it had to be a big one because once Mom died, Jenny and her husband took me in and raised me with their two older girls, Clara, and Mabel. They were nice enough as sisters, but didn't pay much attention to me. Part of that was because they were in high school, and after that, they went and moved on with their own lives. Later, after I left, Jenny got real sick and died, and the last time I saw them was at her wake. Lost touch with them. Jenny did me a favor because she insisted I go to school. I think that if she had not been so hard on me in that area, I wouldn't have met Toby. Things turn out funny sometimes.

I went on to high school and was mostly an average student. I always had a job of some kind, and that seemed more important to me, but Jenny said Mom made her promise I would get an education. Don't know if that is true or not, but I believed it when I was young, and it made me finish school. I wasn't the best student, but that wasn't the teachers' faults. I caught on quick, did little studying, and it seemed to me that school was easier than some of the jobs I had.

The high school senior class was mostly girls, and so some luck came my way. There was a stipend to take some college classes that was available to a male senior who had at least a "C" average and showed what was called *promise*. A few teachers got together and thought I should get it. I was sure at the time they were nuts, but since then, I realized they were just desperate to give it out and not have it wasted. It wasn't much, but paid for a small room at the "Y" near the Chicago Normal College, with some cash left over for books and supplies and a bit of food. So, not that I planned to or even really wanted to, but I found myself out on my own, living in a room hardly big enough to stand with my arms outstretched, and going to school as a part-time college student. It was pure luck because Jenny's husband was never much of a fan of me, and he told me that I had to get out as soon as I turned eighteen.

I took a class or two here and there, just enough to keep to the letter of the stipend, and got a job working for the college. The college was one that trained teachers to work mostly in the Chicago schools, but I wasn't drawn to being a teacher. The institution turned out to be an interesting place for someone like me. And now comes the hard part, Livie, and the part Toby and I hope you are old enough and smart enough to understand. I suspect you are. Toby and I haven't quite figured it all out yet, but we agreed that we would raise you to accept and honor people who are different or at least feel that way. That's important.

Chicago Normal College is where I met Toby. We ended up in a class together, and I noticed him right away. Actually, all the students, especially the women, did. Toby was like a Greek god in his younger days. He was tall and blonde and had great-looking eyes. Still does. He was always polite and friendly to everyone, and he was well liked. I liked him immediately too.

I don't remember what the class was, but I had to do some research and read something for it at the school's library. I went there one day after I completed my janitorial work. I was in the stacks looking for the book and reached for it at the same time Toby did. That's how we met. We shared the book, and then shared a friendship. I never finished college; it really wasn't for me, but am ever glad I went there and spent time in the library. Funny how libraries fit in all our lives.

When Toby moved back to Everstille, and you have read about that, I missed him. I always had some women friends, and I began to see one or two on a regular basis. Yes, Livie, I like women too, and that's hard to explain. I can't figure it out, so I'm not sure you can either. But I was regularly seeing a woman, Betsy, and was thinking that maybe I could have a normal life. Maybe I could marry Betsy, and settle down with her, and get a full-time job, and feel that I was the same as other men. That was the problem I had. I didn't feel normal, didn't feel like other guys felt. I listened to the college guys talk and knew I had to hide my feelings and actions. I was always afraid of being caught doing something I could be arrested for. Toby already explained that we had to be careful when we saw each other on those weekends he came up to Chicago to visit. So, with Betsy, things were just easier in lots of ways. But I missed Toby, and when he came up, and we talked about me moving to Everstille and what life might be like, I realized that was what I wanted. I ended up coming back to Everstille with him. And living with him and Ruth.

I knew about Ruth. I knew that Toby thought he needed to get married, and she had agreed to. I also knew that Ruth didn't really like me when I came to live with them. Toby had told me about the arguments they had, and it was understandable. My feelings about Ruth were mixed too, and I didn't know what to expect. I didn't intend to stay with them forever, but that changed. Ruth and I had our troubles at first. Then, we became friends. And then more than friends.

I can write about this because Toby and I have discussed it at length. We fought about what happened, and then the three of us argued about it, and it seemed to go on forever. Ruth and I felt guilty, but then again, strangely, we didn't. The peculiarity about it is that the three of us loved each other. I don't think I have ever used that word before. It is easier to write it than say it. We knew the town was watching and listening. Small towns have big ears and watchful eyes. That was one of the reasons Anne and I started a sham relationship, so the town could see and hear, and hopefully, forget their suspicions.

Anne is part of our lives. She always will be. Perhaps it would surprise you to learn that I have discussed marriage with her. Toby and

Anne and I have had many conversations over the past months about that and about her moving in with all of us. Anne has remained insistent about not marrying. She said she is married to her books and the library. Anyway, as she explained, a marriage to me would be the ultimate betrayal of Ruth, and she is probably right. I read Toby's writing and he left out what really happened between Ruth and me. He said it was my responsibility to tell you and to tell you as much as I thought you should know. And I think you should know.

I watched a bird build a nest once. First some twigs and loose hay were laid around making a base. Then, little by little, more small twigs and hay, some hair like substance, and odd-and-ends were placed into the base, and then one day when I looked, it had changed. There was a nest. It had been built with small pieces and slowly turned into a home for the eggs she would sit on and hatch. That was the way it was with Ruth. We tolerated each other, and I was grateful that she let me and Toby be together. We kept our spaces, and I let her have her way around the house because I was just a guest. At first.

I watched as she did things for Toby. His shirts were cleaned, and ironed, and hung up. Then one day, mine were too, and she never asked, but just did. I saw her make the baked apples just the way Toby liked them, and one day I came home to the shortbread cookies I had told her were delicious. Ruth worked the same as Toby and me, and how she got the time to do these little things, I don't know, but she did. There was the time Toby broke the coffee cup he used every morning for his coffee, and in a week or so, a replacement appeared. Apparently, Ruth went to the Emporium in town, and they were able to find one just like it. Flowers from Ruth's garden were placed on the table, and the back porch where we sat and watched the sunset was always swept. I noticed these things. I watched as Ruth brought in her twigs and hay and created a nest. A comfortable, clean, organized, and, to my surprise, happy nest. I began to like Ruth who gradually accepted me. She was always polite and never pouted when, on those rare occasions, Toby and I came out together in the morning from my back bedroom.

I assume you are old enough now to understand the sleeping arrangements. Ruth had the main bedroom downstairs. I slept in the backroom upstairs that was farthest from the main staircase, and Toby stayed in the large bedroom above Ruth's. At least, most of the time. We just naturally had our own spaces. When I moved to Everstille, I realized that Toby and Ruth had separate rooms, and I tried to be as unobtrusive as I could be. We all attempted to give each other privacy, and for the most part, it worked.

One early summer Saturday morning, I looked out the window of my room and saw Ruth working in her garden. She was clearing and weeding and taking care of the flowers and a few vegetables she had planted. I knew she had to work that Saturday, but she weeded and worked with the flowers until she had no more free time. She came into the house, and I heard her get ready to go to the library. Toby was downstairs, and they were talking, and drinking coffee, and asking each other about their day's duties. Toby had to go to the high school for a meeting and then show up at a baseball game in the afternoon. He was often gone during weekends and busy with meetings and such which made for plenty of late nights, but that was what his job required. I waited to come downstairs that morning until they both had left; then, I put on my old work clothes and went out to the backyard to the flower garden.

I saw where Ruth had left off with her weeding. When I had the job at the college in Chicago, part of my duties included keeping the grounds cut and neat, doing weeding and such, so I knew what to do. I started to work and finished the garden. Then I got out the grass mower from the shed and oiled it up and cut the lawn. I raked and swept the cut grass off the walk. When Ruth and Toby came home, I wanted the outside of the house to look neat and cared for. I wanted them to see the yardwork was done, and they could rest and relax. I knew Toby planned on doing the yardwork when he came home, but there was no reason for me not to do it. I needed to show them both that I appreciated their kindness. I especially wanted Ruth to know that I was thankful for her tolerance.

The yardwork became my job. I didn't mind (still don't) because I don't work on Saturdays, am able to do it, and enjoy the task. Ruth still worked in her flower garden, but when she couldn't get to it, she would tell me what needed to be done, and I was happy to assist her. Things between us became pleasanter after that. Then there was that one incident that changed my feelings towards Ruth; that made me see her in a different light.

One Saturday when she did not have duties at the library, Ruth was out in the garden, Toby was at the high school, and I was cutting the grass. I had stopped to clear some of the clumps away from the blades, and out of the corner of my eye, I saw one of the neighborhood girls come around the side of the house. She looked at Ruth who was standing just outside the flower patch looking at her accomplishment and removing her garden gloves. The little girl, it was Amy Jackson, was holding a book in her hands and looking upset. I watched as she came closer to Ruth and stood next to her until she was noticed.

"Hello, Amy. Did you need something?"

Amy took a deep breath and started to talk, but tears began to come down her face. She wiped them away and held out the book in her hands.

"Miss Ruth, I am so sorry. I was reading this book and my little brother came by on his bike and he fell off it and it fell on top of me and the book fell and I tried to catch it and the cover tore off and I am so sorry," and Amy held out the torn book to Ruth.

Ruth took the cover and the book and reached into the pocket of her smock and took out a handkerchief. She handed it to Amy, turned her around, and the two of them went to the back porch and sat down on the steps. I listened as Ruth spoke.

"Amy, accidents happen, and thank you for coming to me with this. It is repairable. There is a way to fix this book and place the cover back on it, so it will be fine. I have a thought. On Monday, after school, can you come over to the library? You and I can repair it together. I'll show you what needs to be done. Then you can take the book home and finish it. How does that sound?

Amy blew her nose and stopped crying. "Really? I'm glad it's not ruined. Yes, I'll be there after school Monday, but I don't need to take the book back and finish it. I've read it three times. It's my favorite."

Ruth looked at the book: *Little Women* by Louisa May Alcott. She smiled and spoke again.

"Have you read the other books by Miss Alcott? If you liked this one, you might like the others."

"I didn't know there were more. This one was really good. I'd like to read the others."

Ruth nodded and then she asked. "What makes this book good, Amy?"

Amy thought for a while and then said, "Well, the story is real. The sisters sometimes fought, and I fight with my sister, so I know how that goes. And it's sad too. Every time I read about Beth dying, I cry. I guess it's just a good story."

Ruth nodded once more. She held the book so that the cover fit over the pages and said, "That's the secret, Amy. A good story is the most important thing. You have discovered the trick to writing. I also cried at

Beth's death, and when a book's story makes you feel strong emotions, then you know it's worthy."

They sat on the porch for a few more minutes talking about other books Amy liked, and Ruth suggested additional reading for her. Then Amy, the stress and trouble she arrived with clearly gone, left. When she got to the corner, she turned and waved to Ruth telling her, "See you Monday." At Ruth's wake, I saw Amy come into the funeral home with her parents. She was carrying a book, and placed it on top of another stack that was being started, and I didn't have to walk over the see that a copy of *Little Women* was there.

I remember standing at the lawn mower and looking towards Ruth. She saw me looking at her, and her grass green eyes met mine, and something changed for us both. At least it did for me. Her gentleness and graciousness with Amy touched me, and I saw another side to her. In hindsight, my feelings for Ruth changed at that moment. But it was months before anything happened between us.

The three of us, Terrence, Ruth, and me, became a real unit, a group. Everstille was, and is, a decent place to live, but it was a big change for me. A real change from living in Chicago where there were so many people and so many problems that most people were just concerned about themselves and their families. I had no family. Just some friends and sometimes a girlfriend, and Toby. But when he moved back here, to Everstille, I wasn't sure we would continue our friendship. He wrote to me often, and I wasn't too good at sending letters back to him. Writing is hard for me. I hope you understand this, Livie. This letter is taking a lot out of me.

When I did move here, folks were friendly to me. But I suspect it was because of Toby's position and Ruth's work. They were important to the town, and I came along on their coattails. When I did get a job at the telephone company, I was glad. I was able to help pay the bills and support myself. Things were good for a few years, and then there was some talk in the town.

At first, Toby told me to ignore it. We hadn't done anything to encourage the talk, but I partly blame our neighbor, Mrs. Wilson. She thought she was a bigwig at the church, being in the Rachel Circle and leading the music and playing for the choirs. She was always saying things like, "Oh, Mr. Douglas, I am so glad Ruth's house is a large one so all of you can fit comfortably in it." And "Oh, Mr. Douglas, I saw that you and Tobias were sitting on the back porch talking late last night. I hope Ruth is not ill and that's why she couldn't join you." She was making insinuations about our relationships and it annoyed me. Toby said she is an unimportant busy-body and to ignore her. Ruth said she wanted to be a big fish in this small pond and to ignore her. She was hard to ignore. Partly because she was not totally wrong.

About the time your mother was expecting you, the three of us had a conversation and decided that the only other person we could trust with our secrets was Anne Rivens. I like Anne. She's friendly and helpful and smart and not all full of herself the way so many people are. We got along good enough. When Ruth and Toby suggested that seeing a woman would help to stop some of the talk and rumors, it was Anne who was the logical choice. So, Anne and I began to go to events as friends. And after a time, we became real friends.

On one of the first occasions we went out together, we had a real serious discussion. Ruth and Toby agreed about what I should say if the time was right, and after a short time, I was sure Anne could be trusted. Ruth and Toby both knew what I was going to tell her. We were trusting her with our lives, and we were right to do that. She was then and still is now, the truest friend we have. I told Anne about Toby and me and how we met at the college. I explained, in as careful terms as I could muster, our relationship. I let her know that I was not moving out of their house, and Ruth knew all about Toby and me. And then, I asked for her help. I suggested that we could be friends and just be seen around town together. She listened and asked one or two questions, and then said she would help in any way she could. I was relieved and thankful to her, and so, our friendship was cemented.

Well, Livie, I guess I have wandered all over these papers and wrote all around the subject, and have finally come to the place I need to be. This is the hard part. I promised Toby I would be honest and tell you about your mother and me. I guess I have talked about everything else but that. I watch you in your crib, holding that doll Anne gave you, and you looking like the sweetest thing, and although I know you will not read this until you are grown, these words are difficult to write. There is no other way to write this: Ruth and I became lovers.

We didn't mean to. We went from *circling each other like cats*, that's how Toby put it, to being tolerant of each other, to being friendly, and then to having stronger reactions. Yes, Livie, I loved your mother. There, I wrote that word again. My feelings for her were what I thought a man should feel towards a woman. I have struggled throughout my life trying to understand and explain myself. I cannot. Or maybe I can. The relationship with Ruth permitted me to feel the way I thought other men did. The emotions I experienced with Ruth were different than those I had with Betsy or other women. They were like the feelings I have about Toby. I know I have no excuse for my actions, but the truth is, I don't regret them. I only regret hurting Toby. Even though he got over it. Or said he did.

Toby was traveling. He was doing some work with different principals and schools and would sometimes be away for part of the week on these trips. At times, he would be gone on a Friday and return on Saturday night. Other times he would not come home until Sunday. The times varied, and Ruth and I got used to having dinner together or sitting on the back porch at night watching the sunset, or working in the garden side by side. Over the years we learned to rely on and help each other, and this was comforting. I have always gotten along with women, and I think this was due to my foster mother, Jenny who was a good sort of person.

Anyway, when Toby was gone on these trips, Ruth and I were together. We went shopping at Clampet's for groceries and sometimes to the Bijou Theater to see a movie on Saturday afternoon when Ruth didn't have to work. During those Saturdays when Toby was gone and Ruth was working at the library, I would try out a new dish for dinner, often including ingredients I knew Toby did not like, just to see how it would taste. Ruth was always willing to try different dishes, and we had fun eating dinners together. We talked about our lives and our beliefs. We grew closer.

One Friday in August, Toby left for a weekend seminar and would be gone until Sunday night. Ruth did not have to work the following Saturday, and we had planned on getting up early and working at the weeding and the flowers and the lawn, and then cleaning up and seeing the new movie at the Bijou. We had asked Anne to go with us, but she called on that Saturday from the library as she was closing to cancel out. Her parents were both sick with a summer cold, and she was going over to stay with them and nurse them through the rest of the weekend.

Ruth and I decided that we would skip the movie. After the weeding, we cleaned up. I made us a light supper, and we ate. Then we did the dishes and straightened the kitchen up together and went out to the back porch to sit and try to catch a breeze. It was a warm August night, but it soon cooled off, and we saw some welcomed rain was rapidly approaching. We went into the house to close the windows and lock up, and then stood there talking about going to church the next day. There was a sudden flash of lightening and some deafening thunder claps, and it surprised both of us, and we jumped. Ruth let out a strange squeal, and we laughed at each other, and then, we kissed. I'm not sure why it happened, but I will spare you the details except to say that we did not get to church the next morning.

I wish I could say there was just that one time, but there was not. Ruth and I finally decided that we needed to end whatever it was we had begun. And by early October, the fall session of school was in full swing, and the three of us were back in our usual arrangement. It seemed as though those times between Ruth and me had never happened. Except, Ruth was expecting a baby. She was expecting you.

Once she was far enough along, she told me, and we had to decide what to do. The truth is always best, Livie. Not easy, but best, and we sat down with Toby and admitted what we had done and waited for whatever pronouncement he would give us. I was even prepared to be thrown out of the house and, if she wanted to, would ask Ruth to go with me. I didn't know what would happen. There were tears and anger and hurt and many, many discussions that night and many nights afterwards. Then things got quiet. For a time, the three of us went around ignoring each other and trying to work out in our minds what to do. And then, somehow, and I am not quite sure how, we came together and talked again and agreed that whatever had happened, whatever Ruth and I had done, something amazing was going to come from it.

We became a unit again. This time we seemed to be even more united because we had a purpose. We would be a family, and the three of us would raise the child Ruth was expecting. To maintain what Toby called *social decorum*, it was agreed that Ruth and Toby would be the legal parents, and I would be "Uncle Terry", and we would continue to live together in the large house where we had all been content for so long. Plans were made for cleaning and organizing and painting the birthing room and the nursery, and Ruth discussed her eventual withdrawal from the library and her possible return in years to come when our child, you, Livie, was in school. That will never happen now.

There was, and is, no doubt about who your father is, Cabbage. For one thing, you only need to look in a mirror to determine that, but before you were born, we did not know what your features would be. The other fact is that Ruth and Toby were married, but it was a marriage in name only. They had never shared any intimacy other that a brief hug and kiss on the cheek. That had been the agreement from the start. I guess it is fair to say that we all knew what our sins and offenses were, and Ruth and I bore most of them.

There is not much more to write. The plans Ruth had for you will not be realized, and Toby and I are poor substitutes for her. Anne is here to help us, though. None of us know a thing about raising a baby and caring for a child. I am going to apologize here and now for whatever stupid things we have done. For mistakes I am sure we will make. At least the ones I am sure to make. The one thing you can be absolutely sure of is that we all, Anne, Toby, and me, cherish you. We have planned and talked about how we should care for you and teach you. Our hope, at least mine is, is that we will not do too much damage in raising you.

When you are grown and read this, there may be other things you want to know. Come to me, and ask. I'll answer. I promise you that. I owe you that much. I am here for you. I hope you know this by now, but, Olivia, all my love is yours. That word is easy to write when it comes to you. I will practice saying it to you too.

Uncle Terry

(Terrence Douglas, your father)

Anne Rivens: One Last Thing

One Last Thing

The last true conversation I had with Ruth was the day before she had the baby; three days after our conversation, she died. It was a Friday and the high school was getting ready for the Spring Festival weekend. The weather was perfect, and the entire town participated in this yearly event, making it a celebration for all, staring with the Pep Rally and a Varsity-Faculty baseball game Friday night, and continuing into Saturday when there would be a parade and a nighttime dance for the entire town, not just the high school students. Most of the businesses were closing early, and I was closing the library at noon. There were only a couple of people there, and once they left, I telephoned Ruth. I had been busy with the library's renovation and during the last month, had not been able to spend much time with her. That is something I will always regret.

"Hello," she answered, and I could tell from her voice she was not feeling well. She sounded weak and breathless.

"Hey, how about some company? I am closing the library and can be over in about ten minutes. Do you need or want anything at all?"

"Oh, Anne, I don't need anything, but some company would be great. The front door is open, so come on in."

"Fine. See you soon."

Their house was not far from the library, and I could have walked, but I locked up the building, got in the car, and drove over. I pulled into the driveway and noticed that the grass needed cutting, and wondered if Terry would be able to get it done before the festivities. I walked up the steps, knocked loudly on the front door, and went in calling out, "Hello, it's me."

Ruth was sitting on the sofa in the parlor. Her feet were resting on a foot stool, and she was covered with a blanket even thought it was a warm spring day. She was never a large woman, but the baby made her look enormous and puffy. Her feet and legs were swollen, and as I leaned over to kiss her cheek, she felt both feverish and cold. She was drawn and pale, and there was no proverbial glow to her, no Madonna-like mien. Ruth simply looked desperately ill.

"Hello, Anne. I'm glad to see you. It's been a difficult day, and I suspect this baby will be here soon. My back aches terribly, and I have periodic sharp pains in my lower abdomen. Sometimes it's difficult to breathe. Come here. Sit down. Let's talk. It seems like forever since we were able to spend some time alone. I've missed seeing you."

I stood back and crossed my arms. I was worried.

"Ruth, are you in labor? I can call the doctor. I know Toby or Terrence or both would be glad to come home. Should I make those telephone calls?"

"No, no phone calls. I spoke to Doctor Grenville earlier, and he is aware I am probably in early labor, and it's about time! However, these are only spasms, and he did say that first babies generally take some time, so I am just trying to be comfortable. Toby called and so did Terry, but I told them both to continue with what they were doing, that you were coming over, and if something happened, they would get a telephone call. You know how busy Toby is on this weekend. I am better now that you are here. Sit down."

"Can I get you something to eat? How about some tea?"

"I'm not at all hungry, and my stomach aches. I don't think I could keep anything down. I haven't been able to all day, but, Anne, tea would be nice. Put a bit of honey in it. You know the way I like it."

I left her and went into the kitchen and made the tea. I brought a cup back for both of us and placed them down on the side table within reach. I leaned over to straighten out Ruth's blanket, pushed the lock of her hair that always seemed to be there, back from her face, and sat down beside her.

"Don't fuss," she said. "I'm feeling better. Doctor Grenville said to just take it easy today and if regular pains start, I need to begin timing them. But these aches aren't particularly regular. I'm not even sure they are contractions. Now, Anne, tell me, what are you reading now? We haven't discussed a book in so long. Is there something new the library needs to order? How is the new building going? When will all the moving take place? I miss being there. I miss seeing what's going on and am looking forward to visiting the new building with the baby."

Ruth had encouraged me to order some periodicals for women, and they had recently begun to arrive. I told her about the new wooden magazine racks that were delivered. I explained the ongoing completion of the new library, the moving plans for the furniture and books. I named some of the new novels which had been delivered and were stacked in boxes behind the Circulation Desk. We talked for a while about Mary Renault's book, *The Charioteer,* which I was sure would cause some concern once its theme was discovered, and we laughed at that. Our private joke. As we spoke, I watched her face for any pain that might show up, but except for a periodic minor facial contortion or two, she seemed to be fine. We sipped the tea, and after about an hour, fell silent.

Ruth leaned her head back and sighed. She remained still for a few minutes, and I thought she might have fallen asleep, but she spoke to me with her eyes closed.

"Listen, Anne, I need to ask you something. If during the next day or so, something bad were to happen…"

"Stop, Ruth; you are going to be fine."

"Yes, but I just need to say this," and she opened despondent green eyes and looked at me, "if something happens, I know this baby will be taken care of, but I want you to do something special for me and for this child."

"You know I will do anything."

"Teach him or her. Take this child under your wing, and do for him or her what I did for you. Teach this child to love books. Discuss reading the way we have. Let him or her figure out the messages, the lessons that books hold for us. I know that the baby will be safe and taken care of, but Toby will be busy with his duties, and Terry…"

"Yes, Ruth, I will promise to do that, but you will be here to manage it yourself. I know it. You're just being a nervous first mother, and that's understandable. Wait until the second one comes along. You really will be busy."

I grinned at her hoping to draw her into a happier frame of mind. I was more worried than I let on. I had done some research and reading about older mothers and their travails in childbirth, and I was alarmed about her having this child at home, but she insisted on it. The last few times I had seen her, I thought she seemed to be in distress, but she claimed to be fine. Doctor Grenville checked her weekly, and found no issues. Ruth maintained she was well, and the baby was normal and active, although he or she was overdue. I thought Ruth should be in the hospital for the delivery, but she was unrelenting about having the baby here in the house she had come to love. I scrutinized her paleness and observed her listlessness. There was an angst in my center and a disturbance in my core I could not identify. I needed to tell her something.

"Ruth, I know I have told you this before, but I owe you so

much. I can't thank you enough for mentoring and teaching me. You have done such an amazing job with my informal education that I feel as though I really did go to college. You will be a wonderful mother, and this baby will be smarter than either one of us."

Ruth smiled, and then, suddenly, her smile changed into a grimace. She let out a small moan and closed her eyes. She placed her hands around her stomach and held it, taking some deep breaths and then, eventually, relaxed.

"Are you O.K.? Should I call the doctor or Toby?"

"I am fine. Just a sharp pain."

We were quiet. Then she spoke.

"Anne, you have done so much reading, and that was your habit long before I came here. Have you ever thought of writing? That is often a natural consequence of a lifetime of reading. You have such a great imagination, so much more active than mine, and I think you could be a respectable writer, a noble writer."

"Writing? Write what, Ruth? I don't know what there would be to write about. It seems to me that all the good plot lines have been taken. What could I possibly write in a book?"

Ruth looked at me and smiled. This was a smile I remembered. It may have been her last true smile. She reached over and patted my hand and kept hers on top of mine, enfolding it.

"Well, you know what they say. Write about what you know. If you were to write about the things you have experienced and noticed and lived, that would make the best story. And remember, Anne, it's the story that counts. That was the first thing I taught you. The first question to ask about a book is: *Does it tell a good story?* Remember?"

"Yes, of course I remember. That was the very beginning."

"Write about what you know, Anne. Make it true. And honest. Make it a good story."

And this time, Ruth leaned back, sighing, and closed her eyes for a nap. She still held on to my hand, and I did not move it. I would stay with her until either Toby or Terrence came home, and as I watched her sleep, I considered her words. I thought about what she said about writing, but questioned if I had any ability, and wondered if I could tell a worthy tale, a good story. Ideas moved around my mind as my fingers moved around Ruth's hand, and I decided that one day, I would try.

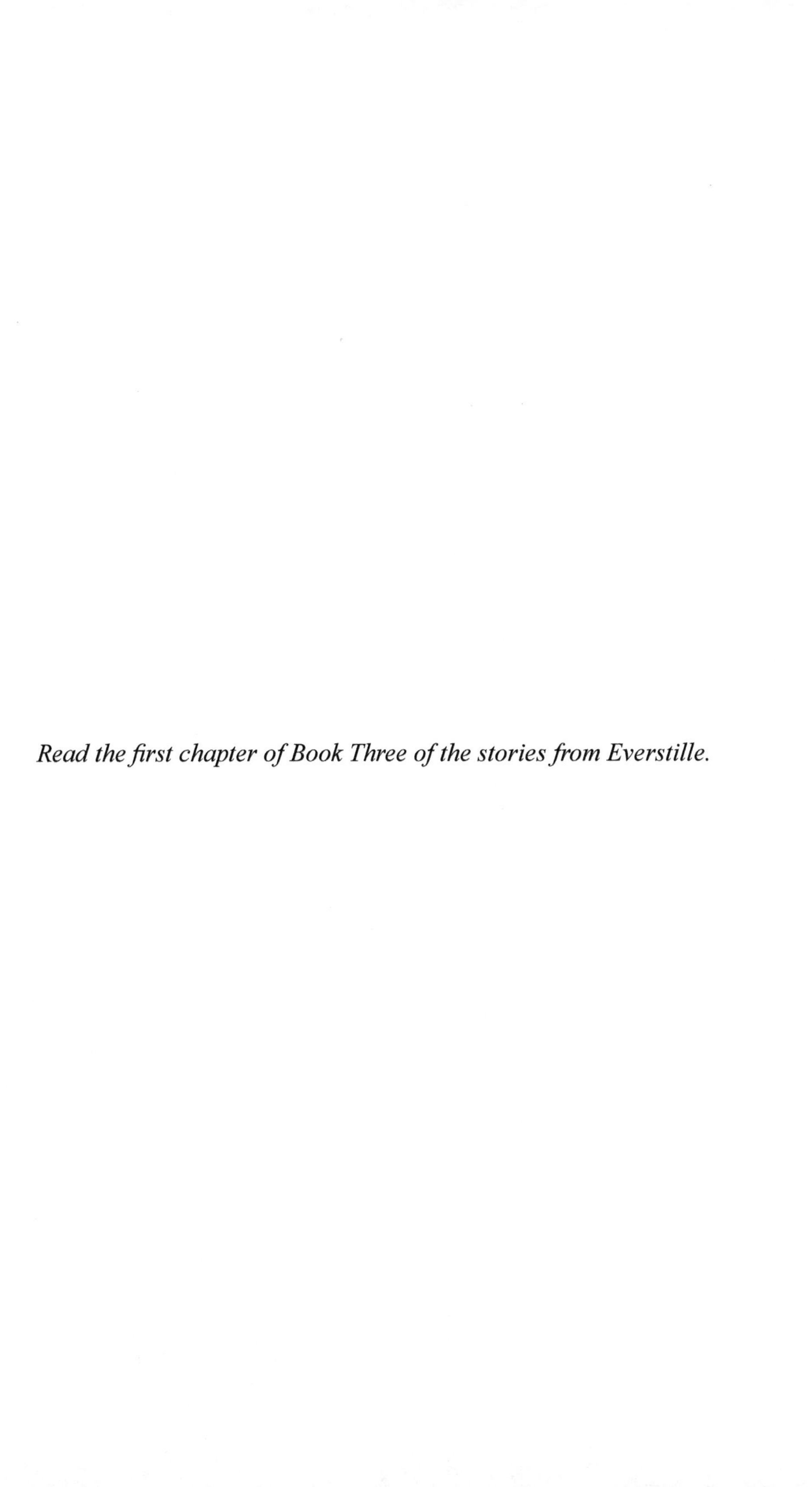

Read the first chapter of Book Three of the stories from Everstille.

0-1 Light Green

My first remembered memory is seeing my mother sitting in the rocking chair in my bedroom, although I did not realize then, she was a ghost. She never spoke, although there was sometimes a small smile on her face. I became used to seeing her rock on the chair Uncle Terry bought for my bedroom and was never frightened. Once I could explain to him or to Dad or to Aunt Anne about what I saw, they assured me it was only the picture of my mother on the small table next to the rocker I was seeing. But I knew better. The one time I described my mother to Aunt Anne, she gave a gasp and held her hand to her mouth. I kept quiet about my mother after that. I didn't want to upset my family.

I don't remember my bedroom walls being a light green color, but I was just born then, and it changed every year, so sometimes the colors are mixed up in my mind. Painting the walls was Uncle Terry's idea although I got to choose the color they would be. I think Dad would have been happy keeping them light green because my mother picked it out, but Uncle Terry explained that color was essential in the world, and we should enjoy all shades offered to us. Since he did most of the work, Dad just let him repaint every year once my new color was selected. As I aged and was able to have a vocal choice in the colors, I enjoyed the changes. I often wondered if the fact that Uncle Terry's hair was such a showy shade of red was why he was so attracted to colors. Of course, mine was the same hue as his.

Mother died when I was born. She lived a day or so and was able to hold me and kiss me, and both Dad and Uncle Terry said she gave me an entire lifetime of love during the briefness we were together. My family entertained me with stories of my mother, and my infancy, and my youth, and that is how I know all these things. They explained again and again what a wonderful woman my mother was and how smart she was, and how loved she was. I believe all those things because, why wouldn't I? After all there is the room in the town library called the **Ruth Evans Pinkerton Room** after my mother, and all the books in there are called *Ruth Books*. My mother was Head Librarian of the Greenwood Library for many years, and she was influential and valuable to the town. I have often been told the story about how friends and townspeople came to her funeral bringing copies of their favorite books which she had encouraged them to read. The books were piled up, stacks of them placed around Jameson's Funeral Home room; they were later to be christened the *Ruth Books*. Aunt Anne told me about the book she offered and why she placed *Oliver Twist* on my mother's casket, and how she would guide me through the reading of it when I was older. That never happened because of what occurred when I was ten, but since then I have read the book. Aunt Anne sent it to me for Christmas when I was thirteen along with a letter. Unfortunately, I didn't get the letter until some years later when I found it with the others.

I loved my years growing up in Everstille with my family. Dad and Uncle Terry and Aunt Anne and I were happy together. Even though Aunt Anne didn't live with us, she was not far away. Her apartment on Charming Lane was not far from our big house, and there were many times I spent the night there. Often on Friday nights if Aunt Anne didn't need to open the library on Saturday, I would stay with her. We would walk to the Emporium, and she would let me pick out a new Golden Book if there was one, and there usually was. Before I was able to read, she would read them to me while I sat in her lap. She pointed out the colors on the pages, and I listened to her soft voice purring the words. Then she would ask me questions about the story, and we would talk about the tale just read. Once I learned to read, our roles reversed, and I would examine her understanding of the story and pictures. At night in her apartment, we played card games, and she showed me how to bake cookies. Before she took me back to my own house Saturday afternoon, we would walk to town, and she would let me pick out a dessert at Peterson's Bakery to enjoy after Sunday dinner. I treasured time with her.

I adored being with Dad and Uncle Terry too. Uncle Terry was more adventurous than Dad, and he and I played in our back yard whenever we could. Dad would sit on the white-washed back porch and watch us throw a ball back and forth, or weed the brightly ornamented flower garden, or play hide and seek in the avocado-colored bushes fencing the property line. Uncle Terry was easy to find because of his hair. I suppose I was too, but he pretended he had trouble and would stand directly in front of me, yelling my name and complaining out loud that this time I had found the perfect place to hide. When he did find me, he would pick me up and throw me over his shoulder and yell at Dad, "Well, now what should we do with this bag of cabbages?" I would laugh and scream and Dad would say, "Terry, be careful; She's the only bag of cabbages we have, and doesn't cooked cabbage with onion sound delicious?"

Uncle Terry would let me help him do the cooking. He delighted in trying new recipes, and even though Dad's penchant was more along the line of meat-and-potato dinners, he always took at least a small helping of whatever was created. One of the jobs Uncle Terry had before he came to Everstille was as a cook in some restaurant in Chicago, so he knew how to work with food. He would take me to visit Aunt Anne at the library, and he would look up new recipes and copy them into a small notebook he kept in his pocket. On Sunday afternoons, Aunt Anne would come over, and we would have a big dinner (always a meat- and- potato type just for Dad), and then we would all help clean up. If the weather allowed, we would go for a long walk around the town and then return to eat the dessert purchased from Peterson's Bakery. We spent the rest of the late afternoon playing games, and after my bath, Aunt Anne would read me a book and tuck me in. Dad said that was Aunt Anne's own time with me, and it was exclusively hers.

Dad helped me with my schoolwork when I didn't understand something. He used to be a teacher but then became the principal at Everstille High School, and was excellent at explaining when I was confused about a math problem or the sentences I was required to write. He was better at clarifying than some of my teachers, and I think that is why school was undemanding for me. When it was Dad's turn to tuck me in, he would often tell me something about Mother…something I didn't know. Once he told me about how they first became friends when he was a teacher and wanted his students to use the library for an assignment and how Mother helped him with the planning. He told me about the times they would chaperone the school dances, and how, when she could, Mother would attend the swim meets because he used to be the swim coach. He described Mother's eyes as "unusually green like the late summer grass", and how she kept her brown hair pulled back in a knot and how one lock always fell across her face. While I loved these stories, I always saw Dad's eyes which were azure colored, become wet. They looked like tiny oceans when this happened.

I loved my childhood. There were friends, and church activities, and summer adventures, and the first ten years of my life were magical. I was happy with Dad and Uncle Terry and Aunt Anne. My life was joyous and pleasurable. And then one day everything I thought I knew changed.